e Files: Collected Short
rime Stories Volume 1

Rachel Amphlett

Case Files: Collected Short Crime Stories Volume 1 © 2022 by Rachel Amphlett

This is a work of fiction. While the locations in this book are a mixture of real and imagined, the characters are totally fictitious. Any resemblance to actual people living or dead is entirely coincidental.

The Case Files short story series

Nowhere to Run (A Detective Kay Hunter short story)

Blood on Snow (A Detective Kay Hunter short story)

The Reckoning

The Beachcomber

The Man Cave

A Dirty Business

The Last Super

Special Delivery

A Pain in the Neck

Something in the Air

A Grave Mistake

The Last Days of Tony MacBride

The Moment Before

All Night Long

1 3 1803165 2

Contents

Contents

Case Files: Collected Short Crime Stories Volume 1

Preface

The idea for the Case Files series of short mystery stories was born from a love of the genre that dates back to my early days of reading and writing.

The first short stories I fell in love with were written by Stephen King, Richard Matheson, Rod Serling and Roald Dahl.

Theirs were the short stories where the good guys didn't always win, where I found myself smiling at what the bad guys (sometimes) got away with, and where often I'd feel a shiver of anticipation as the page turned and the author posed the question "What if?"

After all, what if a contract killer needed to see a chiropractor on a regular basis?

What if a building superintendent took his job a little too seriously when it came to looking after his tenants?

And what if you discovered that your husband was a serial killer?

What would you do?

I hope you enjoy reading the stories collated here – I know I've enjoyed writing them.

Rachel Amphlett
October 2022

Introduction

A brief description about each of the short stories you'll find in this collection follows.

The Reckoning

The newest arrival at a care home for the elderly carries an air of mystery that even a jaded ex-WW2 Resistance fighter can't resist trying to solve.

Then matters take a sinister turn…

A Grave Mistake

A walk in the woods takes a dark turn for Ben…

The Beachcomber

Staying at a tiny guesthouse in Cornwall after the summer, Julie spends her days combing the beaches, looking for things to collect while hiding from her past. Then a storm breaks, and suddenly she's scared. Because you never know what might wash up on the beach…

The Man Cave

When Darren regains consciousness in a dank basement, escape turns out to be the least of his worries…

A Dirty Business

When Michael arrives at work early one winter's day, he discovers that he's not the only one who's had a busy morning…

The Last Super

Larry's been the supervisor of the apartment block for as long as the tenants can remember. And he knows all their secrets…

Something in the Air

When Amy boards her flight to Cairns, it's not by choice. Because it's not just the turbulence that's giving her cause for concern…

Special Delivery

All Jackson Dark wants to do is get home and surprise his wife with the special gift he's bought her…

A Pain in the Neck

Vanessa loves her job as a chiropractor, except sometimes her work takes an unexpected twist…

The Last Days of Tony MacBride

Alan O'Reilly has known Tony MacBride since he was a young boy. Now he's helping to bury him…

The Moment Before

After Ray Holden is told by his doctor that his stress levels are dangerously high, he decides to take drastic action…

Nowhere to Run

When a series of vicious attacks leaves the local running community in shock and fear, newly qualified detective Kay Hunter is thrust into the middle of a fraught investigation.

Determined to make an impression on her first assignment with the murder team, and desperate to stop a cold-blooded murderer before another victim is taken, she may be in danger of risking it all before her career has even started.

A killer is out hunting tonight, and Kay could be the next target…

The Reckoning

Chapter One

The morning before the murder, a late autumn sky laden with rain clung to the rolling hills surrounding the town, the outlook oppressive and grey.

Oak and ash leaves turned from burnt orange to shades of ochre and yellow, littering the pitted asphalt surface of the driveway. They fluttered on the ground in the wind, struggled to become airborne one final time and then sank, defeated by the effort, before being crushed under the wheels of a sleek black car as it braked to a standstill outside the Georgian house.

Sadie Thorp hovered at the portico of the converted manor house with one hand on the open door, the other smoothing down her shirt, the collar stiff from newness and the nursing facility's embroidered blue logo bright above her left breast.

She finished adjusting her short ponytail, peered at the rear smoked-glass windows of the car, and wondered if its passenger was staring back at her.

A moment passed, the *tick tick* of the engine cooling

the only sound until a song thrush burst from the ivy that wound its way up and over the portico, shattering the peace.

The driver's door opened and a uniformed man in his early fifties climbed out.

He had all the bearing of an ex-military man, straightening his navy jacket before moving to the rear and opening the door, his close-cropped hair unaffected by the stiff breeze.

He paused and peered over his shoulder as Sadie called out.

'Mrs Price, it's lovely to see you,' she said, biting back confusion, 'but I didn't think we were expecting you until four o'clock?'

A gloved hand emerged from the gloom of the vehicle, accepting the chauffeur's grip.

'Then you are mistaken.'

Sadie swallowed, then fixed a smile on her face.

The smile that Helen, her manager, used when faced with one of their more difficult residents.

And Evelyn Price promised to be one of those, she was in no doubt.

The ex-Forces' sweetheart glared at her over a pair of pink-framed glasses perching on the end of her veined nose, then raised a painted eyebrow.

The effect did nothing to hide the deep wrinkles or rheumy eyes.

'Welcome to Orchard Skilled Nursing Facility,' said Sadie. 'I'm sure you'll be very comfortable here.'

'I should hope so, given the fees.' Evelyn peeled the gloves from her hands and smacked them against her palm as she watched the driver remove her suitcases from the back of the car. 'Don't put those on the ground, they'll get dirty. Straight into the house with them, Duncan.'

'Certainly, Mrs Price.'

Evelyn watched him for a moment, then turned to Sadie. 'Are you going to stand there all day gaping, or are you going to show me to my room?'

'I – of course. Come this way, please.'

She stood to one side to let the woman cross the threshold, noting how Evelyn paused in the middle of the reception area and turned full circle, her gaze lingering on the oil paintings that adorned one oak-panelled wall before she pointed at the blinking red light above a camera fixed above the front door.

'Do you get much trouble here?' she said.

'What? Sorry, no – those are just for our security while we're working on reception.' Sadie gave a small shrug. 'It's a health and safety requirement, that's all. We're quite a distance from the main road, and we're often working in here on our own.'

Evelyn huffed under her breath in response, and Sadie hurried to the reception desk.

'There's just some paperwork to be signed before I show you to your room,' she explained, hearing the note of apology in her voice.

Evelyn shot her a horrified look and took a step back. 'Give that to Duncan. He deals with that sort of thing, not me.'

'Here, let me.' The chauffeur held out his hand and ran his gaze over the forms. 'Everything will be billed to the company as requested?'

Sadie handed him the black biro from her shirt pocket. 'That's right. We only have a post office box number in London for the address...'

'That'll do.' He scrawled his signature beside the two crosses Helen had pencilled in the correct places on the waiver and billing agreements.

'Thank you.' Sadie crossed to the reception desk, opened the bottom drawer and dropped the folder inside before locking it. She gestured to the hallway leading off to the left. 'If you'd like to follow me, the lift to the first floor is this way.'

'I beg your pardon, young lady, but there happens to be a perfectly good staircase over here,' said Evelyn, jutting out her chin. 'I didn't get to my age through lack of exercise.'

'Of course... I didn't mean...' Sadie looked to the chauffeur for help.

'Mrs Price is exceptionally fit for a lady of her age,' he said.

'Even so, will you be all right with the suitcases?'

'Not a bother. I'll take these up now and then I'll be off.'

'Thanks. It's room number four – up the stairs, last one on the right.'

'I hope it's got a garden view,' said Evelyn, beady eyes watching as Duncan lifted her luggage and made his way up the stairs without a backwards glance. 'We did request a garden view.'

'Your room has a beautiful outlook,' said Sadie, wishing she sounded less flustered and glad that Helen wasn't around to observe her embarrassment. 'I'm told it's the best room in the house.'

'I should think so. Not the cheapest place to stay, is it?'

Sadie took a deep breath as the chauffeur returned empty-handed at the top of the stairs, his gait nonchalant as he descended.

'Shall we go up, Mrs Price?'

'If I must.'

The ninety-six-year-old adjusted her handbag strap across her forearm, then replaced her gloves and reached out for the smooth wooden bannister, determination in her eyes.

'I'll see you tomorrow afternoon as arranged, Mrs Price,' said Duncan. He turned to Sadie and lowered his voice. 'Don't worry. She'll be all right once she's settled.'

Sadie exhaled and forced a smile. 'I'm sure we'll get along fine.'

Chapter Two

A wizened hand dropped the net curtain into place, a bronchial cough hacking its way from the man's lungs as he shuffled across to an overstuffed armchair and sank into it with a groan.

Reassuring warmth from the radiator under the window saturated the room, soaking the available air and capturing a whiff of body odour, cheap soap and aftershave that was fast receding under the notes of furniture polish and lemon-scented bathroom cleaner.

A single bed with metal side rails took up the length of one wall, beige blankets and allergy-free pillows plumped and ready to cushion the old man's form.

Sadie finished vacuuming, made sure the cable was well away from Alan Hendrick's feet in case he tripped, then pulled the laundry bag from its wicker bin and placed it next to the door.

A familiar rattle of tablets being tipped from a plastic pot filled the sudden silence.

This had become their routine: she would vacuum, he

would watch and wait until she was done to take his heart pills, and then he would offer advice – whether required or otherwise – while she dusted and tidied.

'I have a theory.'

She stamped on the button at the back of the vacuum cleaner and watched as the cable coiled away, the plug bumping across the stain-proof grey carpet before clattering into its burrow.

'A theory about what?'

'Not what, who. Her. The new gal. Evelyn.'

'Do you know her?'

'Never seen her before in my life.'

'How do you know her name, then?'

It was like this with Mr Hendrick. Information had to be gleaned from him piece by tiny piece, teased out of him. He loved to taunt, loved to hold on to facts and snippets of gossip like morsels of food to be shared.

'I overheard you talking earlier,' he said.

'Did you now? She smiled. 'Were you eavesdropping?'

'Certainly not. You were talking loudly.'

'All right, I believe you,' she said. 'So, what's this theory about?'

'How long is she here for?'

'Until tomorrow afternoon. Her usual carer is away and there's nobody around to look after her tonight.'

'I don't think she's sick.'

'What makes you say that?'

'I can tell. A person has a certain way of standing or talking when they're hurt. You can spot the weak ones. She isn't one of them.'

'Well, maybe she needs to rest for other reasons.' She

9

moved to the bed and tucked a stray corner of the soft wool blanket under the mattress. 'Convalescing can be for anything, can't it?'

'You don't know why she's here?'

'Now, Mr Hendrick – you know I can't tell you.'

'Well, what *do* you know about her? There must be something you can tell me to alleviate the inordinate boredom around here.'

'She sang for the troops during the war.'

'The British, you mean.' Hendrick wrinkled his nose as he placed the bottle of pills on a small wooden table beside his armchair. 'I didn't hear her.'

'Too busy blowing up Russian tanks?'

'Did I tell you about that?'

'You did, along with the story about the man who helped you steal the German Kommandant's goat.'

'It was a horrible goat. Worst I've ever tasted. Mind you, my friends in the Hungarian Resistance didn't go hungry that week, at least. Did I tell you about the time…'

Sadie tuned out his words as she sprayed a liberal amount of furniture polish onto a duster and began cleaning the mahogany-framed mirror next to the door. She had only worked at the convalescent home for four weeks but knew all of Hendrick's stories by heart.

Alan Hendrick, once known as Bertalan Hendrich. Hungarian by birth, English by circumstances these past seventy-five years. Sharp as a pin, with a twinkle in his eye.

She ran her gaze over the faded photographs in the silver frames on the windowsill of the wife who had died eight years ago and the two sons who never visited, her heart heavy with pity for the animated man she cared for.

He extracted a pocket watch and glared at the clock on the wall. 'It's two minutes slow.'

'Are you sure?'

'This never lies. Quality workmanship, you see. Made in the 1920s, wound daily, dropped once – and still manages to tell the right time.' He jabbed a shrivelled finger at the offending digital counterpart. 'That, on the other hand, is cheap, poor quality, and—'

'Okay, I'll change it.'

Sadie tugged the clock from its picture hook and toggled the switch that marked the seconds before replacing it. That done, she moved around the room, dusting the arrangement of mementoes the old man had collected on a shelf beside the bathroom door as she hummed under her breath.

'Mind the crystal.'

'I will.' She picked up the nearest piece, the green and blue stemmed glass catching the light from the table lamp next to his armchair. 'It's beautiful.'

'It's Überfang. No two are the same.' His voice held a sense of wonder as she turned the glass in her hand.

'Was it a gift?'

'Of sorts.' Hendrick shuffled against the cushions, his eyes shifting to the window.

Sadie replaced the glass, wiped a smudge of dust away from the corner of the shelf, and turned back to him. 'Was it from when you were in the Resistance?'

'Yes.' He waved his hand in front of his face as if to chase away the memories. 'A long time ago now.'

He was tiring.

She could hear it in his voice, see it in the way his eyelids fluttered.

It was often the case after he took his medication.

She pulled the vacuum cleaner towards the door and shoved the furniture polish and dusting cloth into the front pocket of her protective apron.

'Are you warm enough? Do you want me to turn up the heating in here?'

'No. I'm fine, dear. Are you working tonight?'

'I'm on call, yes.'

'That's a shame. You should try the Palinka sometime,' he said. He pointed to a dusty bottle on the shelf next to the glassware, then winked. 'It will, as you youngsters say, knock your socks off.'

Sadie laughed, stooping to pick up the laundry bag.

'I'll pass, thank you, Mr Hendrick. I have another room to clean yet.'

Chapter Three

A subdued quietness filled the old house as Sadie closed the door to room number three and paused on the landing.

An eighty-year-old by the name of Roger Sanders occupied number two, and as Sadie raised her hand to knock, she heard soft snores emanating through the woodwork.

She checked her watch, the dial glinting under the soft hues of the spotlights in the ceiling.

Mr Sanders was known for his afternoon siestas, which had a habit of playing havoc with the cleaning schedule from time to time.

No matter – she would try to return later if time allowed.

Opening a covered hatch beside a fire exit, she swung the laundry bag down the metal chute, then glanced over her shoulder at the faint sound of music.

The distant notes of a swing band filtered from further along the carpeted corridor, the song a reminder of dancing around in her grandmother's kitchen while she listened to stories about rations and air raids.

Sure that the music came from Evelyn Price's room, she peered at the roster of tasks on her clipboard and noted it was almost time to change the woman's dressings.

She rolled her shoulders, heard a satisfied *crick* as a muscle relaxed, and pulled the vacuum cleaner along to the store cupboard, humming under her breath as she collected disposable gloves and a fresh crepe bandage.

Knocking once before turning her key in the lock for number four, she smiled as the music ended and the familiar crack and hiss of a well-worn vinyl record filled the silence.

'Excuse me, Mrs Price. It's time for me to change the dressing on your ankle.'

The nonagenarian stood next to the smaller of the two suitcases the chauffeur had brought in from the car, the open lid exposing a miniature record player with built-in speakers. She held a dull green paper record sleeve in her hand.

'I thought you were coming in here to tell me to keep the noise down,' she said, lifting the needle from the vinyl.

Sadie put down her clipboard beside a half-full water jug. 'Not at all – I like it actually. It reminds me of my grandmother. She used to play that sort of music all the time. I think it reminded her of dancing with my grandfather when they first met.'

'Are they both gone now?'

'My grandfather died before I was born, and I lost my grandmother about ten years ago.'

14

'It catches up with us all eventually.' Evelyn tucked the record into its sleeve, slipped it into a pocket next to the deck and then wandered over to the solitary armchair beside the window. 'Did your grandmother play my songs to you?'

Sadie shook her head. 'I'm sorry, Mrs Price. I haven't heard any of your songs.'

'Well, I suppose you are a bit on the young side.' The old woman sighed. 'And you can call me Evelyn. Mrs Price makes me feel even older.'

'Thank you.' Snapping on the protective gloves, she crouched next to the woman and gently lifted her foot into her lap, setting the new bandage to one side. 'What sort of songs did you used to sing?'

'I never had any of my own – I was too young. The songwriters were busy with the likes of Doris and Vera. I sang some of theirs and the other popular ones.' Her eyes gleamed. 'Occasionally I sang some of the bawdier songs that were around. It depended on the audience. Anything to take the soldiers' minds off what was going on around them for a little while.'

Sadie smiled. 'You must have had such a time of it. Do you still sing?'

'Oh, just for the usual anniversaries. I seem to get rolled out for all of them – the Diamond Jubilee, D-Day, VE Day. Any excuse, and off we go again.'

'Do you enjoy it?'

'It's such a bother these days.' Evelyn scowled. 'All the security arrangements and waiting around while they check this, check that. It's different now.'

'I suppose it has to be. It's all for the right reasons, isn't it?'

The woman wrinkled her nose. 'So they tell me, although if they saw what we got up to back then... I used to get sent over to Belgium, France, wherever else they needed me back in the day. Flak in the skies, anti-aircraft guns on the ground...'

'It must've been dangerous.'

'It was.' A smile flitted across the woman's face for a moment.

'Helen, my manager, said that she'd heard you did some acting as well.'

'I was always a good actress.' Evelyn peered into the encroaching darkness beyond the window. 'I loved that more than the singing.'

'Were you in any films?'

'None that you would have heard of, no.'

Sadie dropped her gaze to the woman's ankle as the last remnants of dressing loosened, and gasped at the purple-yellow bruising that dappled her skin. 'What on earth did you do to yourself?'

'I'm ninety-six, young lady.' Evelyn's mouth twisted. 'I forget I don't move as quickly as I used to. Turned my ankle, that's all.'

'This is a nasty cut.'

'Hence why they're insisting I rest. Not serious enough for the hospital, but they don't trust me to be left at home on my own.'

'No family?' A silence stretched out as she wound a fresh dressing around the woman's ankle, and Sadie bit her lip. 'I'm sorry. I shouldn't ask.'

A sigh tickled her hair as she worked, head bowed.

'I don't have any family, no. People like Duncan are the closest I have to family now.'

Chapter Four

A lingering aroma of roast chicken dinner and steamed vegetables filled the residents' dining room.

Plates clattered in a sink, the noise echoing through the door from the kitchen while Sadie wiped down tables, shuffled chairs and cleared away the last of the unused cutlery.

She glanced up as Helen bustled into view, a clipboard in her hand while she ran through a checklist of items and worked her way around the room.

'How's our newest temporary resident getting on?' she said. 'Settling in all right?'

'Evelyn? Fine, I think. Nasty cut on her ankle.'

'Apparently she tripped and fell.' Helen scratched her pen across the checklist, then tossed the clipboard onto the nearest table. 'Right, that's that done.'

Sadie gathered the last of the cutlery into her fist. 'She hasn't got any family to look after her. A bit sad, given all she's done over the years for veterans.'

Helen lowered her voice. 'According to the woman

who phoned to make the booking, Evelyn's husband died at the beginning of the war when they were both in their early twenties. She never remarried – she put all her effort into entertaining the troops around Europe and then once that was over, she got involved with different charities. Travelled all over the world as an ambassador for one of the big ones.'

'Evelyn said people like her driver are like her family. Seems surprising, given how frosty we were told she could be. She's been all right with me once we got over the initial introductions this morning.'

'She spoke highly of you earlier when I popped in to say hello.'

'Did she?'

'Says you have good taste in music.'

'She was playing some of the records my grandmother used to have. It brought back memories.'

Helen opened the top drawer of a mahogany side cupboard that ran half the length of the dining room wall as Sadie wandered over with the clean knives and forks. 'I'm impressed with the way you build up a rapport with the residents.'

Sadie smiled. 'It's funny – I always thought I wanted to work in accident and emergency when I first started studying to be a nurse, but this seems so much more... satisfying.'

'It takes a certain kind. Speaking of which – I heard Alan Hendrick was chatting you up earlier.'

'I enjoy listening to him. He was a hero, wasn't he? Working with the Resistance and all that.'

'A hero with an overactive imagination,' said Helen,

not unkindly. 'I'm not sure how many of those escapades were his or someone else's.'

'Still, if it wasn't for people like him—'

'Help!'

Sadie jumped at the shout from the residents' lounge, took one look at Helen's face, and ran towards the noise.

When she entered the room, Alan Hendrick was sitting in one of the chairs facing the television, his hands splayed on each of the arms, his face stricken.

Roger Sanders was leaning over his walking frame towards Hendrick, his face puce with rage as he shook a fist at him.

'You stole it,' he snarled. 'It is not yours.'

He held up a gold pocket watch and swung it on its chain, then slipped it into the pocket of his cardigan.

Hendrick's eyes found Sadie's, his expression pleading as she and Helen hurried to his side.

'Don't be ridiculous, Sanders,' he pleaded. 'You've completely lost the plot. Give it back – it's mine.'

'Now, now, gentlemen.' Helen rested her hand on Sanders' arm. 'Roger, did you remember to take your tablets this afternoon?'

Sanders shoved his hands into his cardigan pockets and lowered his chin. 'I don't remember.'

'All right, let's have a look at this watch.'

Helen held out her hand, her voice calm as if she was dealing with a pair of bickering teenagers instead of two old men.

Sanders withdrew it from his pocket, his mouth down-turned. 'It's mine.'

Turning over the watch between her fingers, Helen's

gaze slipped to Hendrick then back. 'Mr Sanders, I'm sorry but I think you're wrong. I've seen Mr Hendrick using this watch on many occasions – before you lived here, too. I believe the watch is his.'

Tears formed in the old man's eyes, and Sadie looked away for a moment, embarrassed for him.

'I don't remember,' he managed. 'I don't remember anything anymore.'

Helen placed the watch on a low table beside Hendrick's chair and sighed. 'Well, I'm sure we can put this all behind us. There's no harm done, after all. Shall we get you upstairs, Mr Sanders? I'll fetch you a cup of tea.'

She pulled Sadie to one side and lowered her voice as they watched Sanders shuffle away, the man stabbing his walking frame into the carpet before each tentative step. 'He'll be fine once I've got him settled and checked his medication. Help Mr Hendrick back to his room, then take your break. With Anna off sick, I'll need you to take turns with me to run the night shift so get your head down for a couple of hours. I'll wake you when it's time to swap over.'

'All right, thanks.'

The creak of the walking frame retreated into the corridor as Helen guided Mr Sanders away from the dining room, and then Sadie wandered across to Hendrick.

'Would you like me to bring you a warm drink?'

'No, that's fine. Thank you. I think I'll go to bed now. This whole episode has left me quite exhausted.' He leaned on his walking stick and eased himself away from the soft cushions, nodding as she cradled his elbow in her palm while he found his balance.

'Don't forget this.' Evelyn crossed the carpet, her face pale as she handed over the watch to Hendrick, her gaze roaming his face while he turned the watch in his hands. 'That's quite a specimen. How long have you had it?'

'It was a gift – from a long time ago,' he said, dropping it into his pocket. He turned to Sadie. 'I suppose you want to come with me to make sure I don't get into any more trouble.'

'Are you going to be all right, Mr Hendrick?' she said as she opened the door to his room and switched on a lamp that gave out a soft glow from its position on the bedside table.

'I suppose so.' He shrugged off his worn jacket, mumbling his thanks as she shook it out and placed it on a coat hanger ready for the morning. He lowered himself to the armchair beside the window as she drew the curtains, his nose wrinkling. 'It isn't the first time he's threatened me, you know.'

'Really?' Sadie couldn't help the surprise in her voice. 'Why on earth would he do that?'

'It's either his dementia or the tablets he's taking.'

'That's awful.'

As she tucked a blanket around his legs and helped him put on his suede slippers, Hendrick managed a smile and held up his walking stick.

'Don't worry, petal. If he tries anything again, I'll whack him with this. That'll teach him.'

'I'd much rather you pulled the emergency cord, Mr Hendrick. Good night.'

22

Chapter Five

A comforting gloom had descended on the office by ten-thirty and, after a taking a break as Helen had suggested, Sadie was content to work in the warm light from her desk lamp that counteracted the glare from her computer screen.

She signed out of her personal email account, closed the window, and returned to the health and safety report she was typing up for Helen in relation to the altercation between Hendrick and Sanders.

Eyeing the growing amount of paperwork stacked in the tray beside the screen, she resolved to take care of the filing first thing tomorrow. The metal cabinet drawers that lined the wall behind her chair tended to rattle and scrape, and it would do no good if the residents complained about the noise while they were trying to sleep.

Humming under her breath, the memory of her grandmother still fresh in her mind, she rubbed at tired eyes and reached out for the mug of coffee next to her keyboard.

When she'd seen the job advertised at the nursing

facility, she had approached it as a stepping stone – a way to gain some work experience to lend weight to the paper qualifications that sat in her personnel file in another locked cabinet under the windowsill to her left.

However, only a few weeks into the role, she could understand why people chose this as a vocation. Some of their residents were only short-term visitors, like Evelyn Price, but others had nowhere else to go. It seemed to her a harsh reality that in their time of need and despite what many of them had done for their country during the war and afterwards, they had been discarded by society.

People like her and her colleagues kept them safe from the harsh world beyond the ornate gardens of the nursing facility.

She pulled up the sleeves of her sweater, wondering if she should turn the thermostat down the next time she conducted her walk through the silent building. It was a fine balance between keeping their guests comfortable and not melting while on the job.

Putting the coffee aside, she exhaled and vowed to finish the report before eleven o'clock and the rostered changeover. At least that way, Helen could read through it when they switched.

She reached into her bag and pulled out a muesli bar, a small snack to keep her going until it was her turn to head upstairs to the twin room she shared with her manager.

It was a simple set-up – whoever was rostered for the night shifts shared a room on the second floor, away from the reception area in order that a few hours' sleep could be taken in between keeping an eye on the residents and catching up with the administrative work.

Working four days in a row at a time, Sadie had become adept at packing the small suitcase she used for work. When she had first started, she had rather optimistically placed a paperback book inside – the reality was, the moment her head hit the pillow, she was asleep until her alarm went off the next morning.

She raised her head as a red flashing light appeared on a panel above the computer screen.

There was no warning, no audible siren, but the light meant that Alan Hendrick had pulled the emergency cord in his room.

Checking that her set of master keys was clipped to her belt, Sadie snatched up the mobile first-aid kit next to the office door and raced towards the stairs, her footsteps muted by the carpeted treads.

When she reached the landing to the first floor, Evelyn and another resident – Mrs Taylor – were standing outside their doors, their faces bewildered.

'I heard a crash,' said Mrs Taylor, her voice trembling.

'Excuse me, ladies.' Sadie didn't wait for their response, brushed past them and inserted her key into the lock on Hendrick's door. 'Mr Hendrick – Alan – is everything okay?'

A crumpled form sat against the nearest bed leg, and as Sadie reached out to her left and slapped the light switch, she blinked before dropping to the floor.

Alan Hendrik looked up at her, his eyes bewildered, the red emergency cord tangled around his fingers.

'There was somebody in my room.'

Sadie peered at the window, but the curtains were still

drawn closed and no wind billowed the material away from the glass.

'Let me take a look at you. Did you fall out of bed? Are you hurt anywhere?'

'I'm fine,' he snapped. 'I stumbled over the corner of the blanket when I got up to see who it was. I must've been half asleep and tripped.'

'There was no-one else here when I came in, Mr Hendrick.'

'There was someone here, I tell you!'

'The door was locked,' said Sadie, keeping her voice calm. 'No-one's been in here. I've got the only other key.'

'What if someone took your key? What if someone got into the house when you weren't looking?'

'I can assure you, all the doors downstairs are locked as well – and if someone had come to the front door, I'd have seen them on the cameras, wouldn't I?'

'I'll bet it was that bloody Sanders. Wanting to steal my things.' His eyes drifted to the wooden shelf and the Überfang glassware before finding her once more. 'He's mad, you know.'

'He's got early-stage dementia, Mr Hendrick, that's all.' Sadie bent over, wrapped her arms under the old man's and coaxed him upright. 'Let's get you back into bed before you catch a cold.'

Hendrick wilted in her arms as she pivoted and sat him on the bed, the mattress sagging a little.

'Maybe I *was* dreaming,' he murmured.

'It must have been very vivid, to frighten you like that.'

'I wasn't frightened.' His chin jutted out. 'I was angry.'

At that moment Sanders appeared at the open door, his hair ruffled, pillow lines across one cheek.

'What the bloody hell is going on?' he asked, sleep coating his words with a bleariness that matched his eyes. 'What's all the noise about?'

'Mr Hendrick called out in his sleep, that's all,' said Sadie, turning her attention back to Hendrick and helping him under the covers. 'It's nothing – best go back to your room, Mr Sanders.'

'Hmmph.' Sanders tightened the belt of his dressing-gown, then shuffled his walking frame around. 'Probably dreaming up more stories about his time in the Resistance.'

Hendrick pushed Sadie's hand away and leaned forward.

'I'll have you know—'

'Leave him,' said Sadie. 'You know what he can be like. You need to rest.'

Leaving the bedside light on and making sure Hendrick had a fresh glass of water within easy reach, she said goodnight and closed the door.

The lock slid into place with a smooth click and after clipping the keyring to her belt, she closed her eyes a moment, wondering if she would get any sleep herself tonight after the fright Hendrick had just given her.

She jumped as a hand wrapped around her forearm and turned to see Evelyn staring at her, her eyes wide.

'Did he say Hendrick was in the Resistance?'

'Yes. Hungary, apparently. He says he saved a lot of lives.'

Rachel Amphlett

Evelyn shook her head, her face crestfallen. Her grip loosened on Sadie's arm before she turned and wandered back towards her room, leaving a trailing scent of lavender in her wake, her shaking voice barely above a whisper.

'The stories we could tell....'

28

Chapter Six

Sadie tugged the brush through her thick brown hair, snapped an elastic band over the ends and fastened her wristwatch as she paced the small staff bedroom she shared with Helen.

Bright sunshine sparkled through the window that overlooked the car park and delivery entrance to the kitchen, and she watched as a cheeky sparrow perched on the sill a moment before it plucked a bug from the wisteria branches that twisted across the brickwork beside the glass and flew away.

Placing her shower gel and hair straighteners into the locker by the side of the single bed she used while on night shifts, she pocketed the key and reached for the door handle before snatching her hand away as it opened.

'Oh.'

'Sorry – I was hoping to catch you before you came downstairs.' Helen waved her back inside and pulled the door closed.

'What's wrong?'

'Alan Hendrick passed away in his sleep last night.'

'What—'

'The local doctor's in his room now, and two people from the funeral home have just turned up.' Helen raised her hands. 'Hell of a way to start the day, I know, but…'

'When did you find out?' Sadie sat on the end of her bed, trembling.

'About an hour ago when he didn't show up for breakfast. Rosie's on reception this morning, and went up to find him.' Her shoulders sagged. 'He was in his armchair, next to the window.'

Sadie sniffed, then pulled out a paper tissue from her trouser pocket and blew her nose. 'He loved to sit by the window and watch the garden. Do you think… do you think he knew?'

Helen gave her a sad smile. 'Perhaps. He looks very peaceful. Would you like to come and say goodbye to him?'

'Is – is that all right?'

'He always said how much he loved chatting with you.' Helen held out her hand. 'Come on. I'll go with you. The doctor's just doing the paperwork so they can take his body away.'

Sadie fell into step beside her as they wandered downstairs to the first floor and along to room number three, her thoughts tumbling.

She'd seen a few dead bodies during her training, but this was different; more personal. Helen was right – he'd enjoyed her time with Hendrick and his anecdotes, however far-fetched they might have been.

'I'm going to miss him.'

'We all are.'

The door to number three was ajar, and the muffled and reverent voices spilling out through the gap fell silent as the two women entered.

Helen was right – Alan Hendrick did look peaceful, his head tilted to one side and his eyes closed.

The doctor had placed Hendrick's hands in his lap, and as Sadie wandered across to where his still form sat in the armchair, she reached out and touched his fingers.

'I'm going to miss you, Alan. And your stories.'

'The paperwork's done,' said the doctor, turning his attention to Helen. 'I'm happy for these two to take him now.'

'Thank you.' Helen's voice floated across to where Sadie crouched, and she straightened as her supervisor gestured to the older of the two men from the funeral parlour. 'Would you like to get him ready?'

Sadie stood to one side as the men unfolded a stretcher and gently lifted Hendrick onto it.

The younger man paused at Hendrick's shoulder, his head bowed a moment before he held out a chain to Helen.

'There's a key on this. Might be for the bureau over there, or something.'

'Thanks. I'll take a look after he's gone so we can make a list of everything.'

The man nodded and then draped a blanket over Hendrick before positioning himself to lift his end of the stretcher.

Sadie opened the door and stepped across the threshold to make way for them. When she glanced over her shoulder, she was astounded to see the other residents from the first floor standing next to the stairs, their heads bowed.

Crossing the landing, she peered over the stair bannister to see the kitchen staff, cleaners and other nurses had done the same, forming an honour guard down the stairs and all the way to the front door.

Helen joined her. 'It's our way of showing our respect on their final journey.'

'It's lovely.' Sadie fell into place beside her supervisor as the two funeral parlour workers passed, the stretcher carrying Alan Hendrick's covered form borne between them as if it weighed little more than paper.

She wiped a tear from her eye as they continued down the stairs, recalling how delicate she'd thought the man as she'd helped him to his feet the night before.

'How about cracking open that Palinka he was always going on about and raising a toast?' Roger Sanders leaned over his walker and leered at the receding figures as they passed from sight.

'That's not appropriate, Mr Sanders, as well you know,' Helen scolded him. 'Now, isn't it time for your medication?'

He grumbled under his breath but acquiesced as one of the day nurses reached the top of the stairs and advanced towards him.

With that the other residents departed, retreating to the privacy of their respective rooms.

Sadie noticed Evelyn lingered on the landing a moment longer, and then the woman gave her a slight nod and turned away.

When she too had gone back to her room, Sadie caught up with Helen.

'What if that altercation with Sanders last night caused Mr Hendrick's heart to fail?'

'I don't think so. The doctor said he showed no sign of stress. Besides, Alan was quite a robust character despite his heart condition.' She exhaled, then gestured down the stairs. 'Go on – the dining room needs to be cleared up now breakfast is finished down there, and you'll have to get Mrs Price ready to be collected at one o'clock this afternoon while I make a start going through Alan's things and cataloguing them.'

'Life goes on,' Sadie murmured.

Chapter Seven

Sadie kept a watchful eye on Roger Sanders as he accompanied his daughter around the concrete path that bisected the landscaped gardens beyond the house.

She shivered, peering up at the grey clouds that shrouded the horizon, threatening rain.

Zipping up the black quilted coat she wore over her uniform, she sniffed the air. At the far end of the lawn, the contracted landscape gardener had started a small bonfire to cope with all the leaves he had raked from the paths around the property.

It would do no good at all if one of their residents slipped and fell.

'We'll be off now.'

Duncan's voice jolted Sadie from her daydreaming, and she turned to see him on the threshold, Evelyn's arm looped through his as she left the reception area.

The chauffeur had already carried the two suitcases downstairs and placed them in the car, the portable record player treated with particular reverence.

'Wait here a moment, Mrs Price,' he said. 'I'll get the door open first.'

'I hope you found everything all right during your stay...' said Sadie, the words dying on her lips. 'I'm sorry. I realise this morning has been traumatic.'

The older woman moved to where she stood beyond the portico.

'It was simply Mr Hendrick's time.' Evelyn looked up at the Georgian façade, her eyes wistful.

'I suppose so. That's what Helen said earlier.' Sadie offered her arm and walked side by side with the woman to the car, nodding to Duncan as he opened the back door. 'I hope your recovery continues to go well, Mrs Price.'

'I'm sure it will. I have a few more appointments to keep, but I'm determined to make every one of them count.'

Evelyn turned and rested her hand on Duncan's outstretched arm before lowering herself onto the back seat.

The chauffeur made sure she was comfortable, then closed the door and faced Sadie, shaking his head.

'An amazing woman,' he said, his voice full of awe. 'Hard to believe she's in her nineties now. Rumour has it she worked for SOE during the war.'

'SOE?'

'Secret Service.'

'But I thought she sang. She said she used to entertain the troops. And act.'

'Oh, she was an actress all right. God knows what she got up to behind enemy lines. They've never done an official count of how many lives she saved. Or killed.'

Sadie blinked, aware that her mouth had dropped open.

The back door to the car opened, a leathery forearm visible in the gap between the hand rest and the darkened interior.

'Duncan? It's time to go. Hurry, or else I shall be late for my next appointment.'

The chauffeur shot Sadie a rueful smile as the door slammed shut. 'You heard her. We'll be off. Thanks for making her stay comfortable.'

Sadie spun on her heel and raced through the front door, up the stairs.

She found Helen in Alan Hendrick's room, standing by the window while she held a faded photograph up to the light.

'I found out who Evelyn was, what she did,' she blurted.

Her supervisor said nothing for a moment and instead turned the photograph around in a shaking hand. 'Hendrick wasn't who he said he was, either.'

'What?'

The image was yellowed with age.

In the background, a high wire fence was secured into place with concrete posts. Behind the wire, skeletal people wearing dirty striped shirts and matching trousers stared at the photographer, their expressions conveying despair, starvation, horror.

In front of the wire fence, Alan Hendrick stood stock-still, his spine rigid.

Sadie's eyes took in the black uniform, the polished calf-high boots, the skull and crossbones cap badge.

He held up a pocket watch on a chain, dangling it so that the light caught the gold casing.

Even with the passing of time, she recognised it.

'Where did you find this?' Sadie took the photograph, afraid that Helen would drop the frame, and stared at the image.

'Locked away in the bureau. There's more,' said Helen. 'Diaries. Lists. Medals he was given by Hitler.'

Bile rose in Sadie's throat as she stared at the young man in uniform.

She raised her gaze to the crystal antiques that lined the shelf and then her eyes fell to the pocket watch on the bedside table, its dials frozen in time.

'He didn't steal the Kommandant's goat, did he?' she managed. 'He *was* the Kommandant. He took all of these trinkets from those poor people.'

'What do we do?'

'I think it's already been done,' said Sadie, dropping the photograph onto the armchair beside the window.

She raised her gaze to the panes in time to see the black car passing the manicured lawn and rhododendron bushes that lined the driveway, the licence plate obscured by billowing smoke from the gardener's bonfire.

Its brake lights flashed once when it reached the gateposts, and then Evelyn Price was gone.

'If that's your name,' Sadie whispered.

THE END

A Grave Mistake

Foreword

An abridged version of *A Grave Mistake* first appeared in *Mystery Weekly* magazine. The unabridged version follows.

A Grave Mistake

It was the sound of his own panicked breathing that scared Ben the most.

A late autumn sun collapsed beneath a line of naked hornbeam and oak, its rays shrivelling against a pale grey Oregon sky that receded through an expanse of tangled branches.

The last tentacles of heat retreated from a dirt path, withered away under rotten ferns and bracken, then surrendered the woodland to damp biting cold.

He tipped back his head and swore, the curse echoing off the thick trunks that surrounded him.

A blackbird scuttled out from under a buckthorn shrub then took flight, its brittle parting cry rebuking him for the disturbance.

Ahead, an algae-covered pond sat nestled within a grove of birch trees, taunting him.

It was their third meeting within the space of forty minutes.

The stench hadn't improved since their last parting.

The rancid aroma from the stagnant water wafted on the breeze, and Ben ran his eyes over the upside-down shopping cart in the middle of it, one wheel missing, the raw wound covered in detritus.

He placed his hands on his hips, exhaled, and then turned his back on the fetid pool once more and took off down the next fork in the path, a renewed urgency in his stride.

This route was narrower, twisted, less used.

The boughs above his head crowded in as if curious to know who walked amongst them.

Hazel saplings poked and prodded at his padded black jacket that looked great, but allowed every cold tentacle of wind to wrap its way around his body as he pushed his way through the thickening undergrowth.

Leaf litter covered the muddy fringes of the path, colouring the route in ochre hues and sticking to leather uppers that glistened with an obsessive shine.

He began to hum under his breath, a tune from his college years to fight against the silence encroaching with every step.

His heart rate quickened at a gap in the trees, the promise of escape.

He hurried, stumbled forward, broke through the branches that barricaded his way.

Then stopped.

In the glade, under a natural arch of oak and ash and accompanied by a choir of flies, was a grave.

Fresh.

Scuff marks scratched the dirt around it, scraped and scoured to create a hole, then backfilled in a hurry.

Dead leaves covered the churned soil, a feeble attempt to hide the secrets beneath.

He circled the shallow mound, his breath escaping in short sharp chokes, panic twisting at his chest.

Ben swallowed.

Somewhere off to his left, a twig cracked, the noise as loud as a shotgun as it echoed amongst the tree trunks.

He bolted for a narrow path leading off to the right that soon became clogged with saplings and tendrils of ivy.

Ben dropped his hands, and with a renewed energy began to swipe at the branches in his way, desperate to find a way through.

Reaching a crossroads in the dirt, he spun around, hands clasped on top of his head, his gaze sweeping left and right.

The late afternoon sun had turned to twilight now, shadows deepening and crawling towards him from the gloom between the undergrowth.

He brought his hands to his mouth, cupped them around his lips and blew hard, then squinted through the trees.

Pausing to pull out his cell phone, he held it aloft and snarled at the screen.

There was no signal here, no way to check his location or work out where he went wrong.

Ben's gaze fell to the path as he shoved the phone back in his pocket.

He froze.

Something had been dragged through here.

Something heavy.

He checked over his shoulder.

The scuff marks continued east, two parallel lines carving an uneven path.

Towards the grave.

Lifting his chin, his eyes followed the scuff marks as they disappeared into the distance, heading west.

Fear turned to desperation – maybe that was the way back to the park entrance.

Maybe that was the way out.

He glanced over his shoulder.

Nobody followed.

He set off, started humming again, a habit borne of nerves.

No birds accompanied him now; no far-off calls and whistles reached his ears.

Afraid to stop, afraid to register the silence that was so alien to him, Ben ploughed on, his pace quickening with every passing second.

He broke into a run, swiping his hands at the thin reed-like saplings, ducking under low branches.

Sweat beaded across his forehead, pooled between his shoulder blades as his lungs heaved from the exertion.

Ben blinked as the trees began to thin out and the path began to widen.

He could hear voices then.

Close, so close.

Just a little farther to go…

Ben stumbled into the clearing beside a sign for car parking, his boots sliding on the gravel surface as he came to a halt and raised his hand to shield his eyes from blinding headlights.

Two uniformed police officers turned to face him, their conversation cut short.

The younger of the two officers rested a hand against his radio as it emitted a squawk, and called out.

'Is this your vehicle?'

Ben ran his hand through his hair, plucked out an errant twig that had caught in his fringe and gulped a lungful of air, his heart hammering.

'Is there a problem?'

Voice calm, he edged closer.

The older officer circled the car, the beam from his flashlight arcing over the windshield, the radiator grille, the license plate splashed with mud.

The younger officer – McLaren, according to the stripe opposite his badge – repeated his question.

'Is this your vehicle?'

'It is. Is the park closed? I got lost.'

Both men took a step back as he put his hand in his pocket, fingers twitching near their weapons.

'Hands where we can see them, sir.' The other one, Thomas, barked the words.

'It's just my keys.' He jangled them, dangling them from his forefinger and thumb. 'I need to get back – my wife will be wondering where I am.'

Their expressions changed then, a flash of *something* flitting across McLaren's features.

'Can you open the trunk, sir?'

Ben fumbled the keys on his first attempt, then aimed the fob at the car and blinked as the indicator lights flashed.

Thomas moved to his side as he reached out for the lid, a hand outstretched. 'Slowly.'

A reluctant sigh escaped Ben, his shoulders slumped as he opened the trunk and McLaren stepped forward.

His flashlight swung over the bloodied blanket, the discarded shoe, the cell phone with its cracked screen.

All hers.

All the things he planned to come back and dispose of once he finished digging the grave.

'What have you done with your wife, Ben? Where did you bury her?'

He choked out a laugh tinged with irony and regret.

'How the hell would I know? I told you, I got lost.'

THE END

The Beachcomber

Chapter One

As soon as Julie saw the thick-set man walking along the desolate shoreline towards her, she knew there would be trouble.

She could sense it, like the incoming lightning storm that filled the air with burning ozone and malevolence, turning the sunset from reddish gold to angry indigo and staining the horizon.

Clenching her fists, inhaling the salt-heavy breeze that whipped her straggly brown hair around her neck and shoulders, she watched while he stumbled across the uneven pebbles and sand with his head down.

He was limping – a swaying motion that pitched him from side to side as if the storm had him in its clutches, unwilling to release him.

Where had he come from?

Scanning the entrance to the footpath she'd followed from the outer edges of the small coastal town, she realised his dogged progress would have taken him straight past it, not along it.

How long had he been walking towards her?

A lone concrete slipway served as the only other access to the sea here, but that was almost half a mile away, next to the council signs about beach safety and a black plastic waste bin with litter scattered on the pavement around it.

Beyond the slipway, terraced houses lined the narrow potholed road that weaved its way along the Cornish coastline.

The buildings jostled for position, whitewashed walls tainted with grey now that the storm was getting closer, their salt-covered windows peering at her from under slate tiles as she stared back at them.

A desolation clung to the place if it was lamenting the end of the summer season and the tourists that had lined its winding streets.

For now, it was shuttered, closed.

Was he staying in one of the half-empty guest houses, like her?

Had he checked in to the same one?

She hoped not.

This place, with its sheltered port and southerly aspect, was meant to be a refuge, designed as an emergency harbour during storms back in the days when ships relied on sails.

She was meant to be safe here, away from trouble, away from danger.

At least for a while.

Scowling, Julie moved closer to the lapping waves, her eyes downcast while she searched.

She didn't want company.

If she were honest, she wasn't sure exactly what she

wanted, but the walk served to give her time to think, to process the jumbled memories and worries that permeated every waking hour when she wasn't scuffing over the sand and weaving between the tideline of dead fish, shells and seaweed.

She raised her gaze at a soft slurp of heavy footsteps and a surprised grunt, then staggered backwards.

She was so lost in thought that she had almost collided with him.

He flinched.

Most people did.

It was a natural reaction given the pitted patchwork flesh of her right cheek, the scars and new tissue angry and pink.

Sore.

Painful.

A natural reaction, except that a little more of her shrivelled away every time she experienced it.

'Burns?' he said, his brows knitting together. 'Nasty.'

She snorted at his directness, at the lack of concern in his voice.

There was a rough edge to it too – cigarettes probably, or perhaps years of shouting over loud machinery.

'Yes,' she said because he was right.

'There's a storm coming, by the look of it.'

On cue, thunder rumbled and shook the briny air – closer this time.

'What are you doing out here?'

He attempted casual but she could hear the worry nibbling away at the edges.

'Looking for stuff. Shells, glass. Things like that.'

'Beachcombing, you mean?'

'Yes.'

'Finding much?'

'Bits and pieces.'

She jiggled the plastic container in her hand, the movement rattling hag stones and shells against pieces of buffed sea glass.

Green and white.

No blue glass yet.

Pushing her hair away from her face, she inclined her head towards the darkening horizon. 'There'll be more in the morning. Usually is, after a storm. You never know what'll get washed up here – or so I'm told.'

Another flash of lightning tore across the sky.

'You're not from around here then?'

'No.'

He tilted his head and narrowed his eyes. 'Do I know you?'

She bit back a nervous laugh. 'I don't think so. Are you a local?'

'No.'

'Oh. What are you doing here?' She watched his expression change from feigned interest to hunted before he looked away, his gaze casting out to sea as if looking for a way to escape.

'I needed to get away for a while.'

Me too.

Julie squinted as the first splodges of rain smacked against her scars. 'I'd best go. It's going to get rough out here by the look of it.'

She managed a small smile, the skin around her mouth tight, new, while her heart rate quickened in fear.

'Look after yourself,' he called after her.

His next words were whipped away as the wind tore at the clouds on the horizon and churned the waves into a foaming mass full of foreboding.

Chapter Two

Julie towelled her hair dry and applied the special cream to her face, wincing as the nerve endings jangled and protested.

Months.

Maybe years, the specialist said.

It depends.

Be patient.

Her hair had grown longer in the ten months since the fire, her fringe now hanging in dark curtains over her cheeks.

She twisted the lid on the grey-coloured plastic pot and placed it beside the bubble pack of painkillers before turning away from the washbasin, tweaking the pullcord for the bathroom light.

A streetlight farther along the lane illuminated the double room she rented, bathing the soft blankets that stretched across the iron-framed bed with a subtle glow.

All the fixtures and fittings were functional, clean, nothing more.

An ancient radiator hugged the wall under the window sill and a small television clung to a bracket above a pitted oak-effect dresser.

She turned away from it, ignoring the remote control that had been placed on top of the dresser.

She hadn't watched television after leaving the hospital in Exeter, too afraid to watch the news and unable to lose herself in serialised dramas that bore no resemblance to real life.

Her life.

She could hear the television through the thin plaster wall from the room next door though, a man's voice calling out at regular intervals. Odd words, a jumble of composers' names, cities, songs...

A quiz show, then.

Was he winning, or losing?

Rain lashed against the window, and she debated a moment whether to pull the curtains or watch the remnant storm as it passed overhead and rattled the roof tiles.

Then she saw him, standing at the top of the concrete ramp leading down to the beach, his body leaning into the encroaching wind.

He tipped his head to one side, and she spotted the minute spark and flare of a cigarette lighter.

The movement was subtle, but enough.

He hadn't recognised her, though.

Had he?

She should've asked his name.

She would've done, ten months ago.

He turned around to face the guest houses, his profile

silhouetted while a final, almost defiant flash of lightning illuminated the coast road.

Julie reared backwards, sure he could see her watching him, but he didn't move, didn't react.

He simply stood, stock-still.

Was he watching her?

Or waiting for something – or someone?

She reached out and swished the curtains closed, then leaned across and flicked on the light above the bed, its beam billowing across the pillows and a dark pink velvet sash that covered the top half of the blankets.

She crossed to a wooden ottoman at the foot of the bed and opened the cheap suitcase that lay on top of it, extracting a well-worn T-shirt.

A favourite.

Something familiar, with the logo of a band embossed across the front that had split up over a decade ago.

A single wardrobe huddled beside the door, but she hadn't opened it since her arrival.

She had lied to the owner of the guesthouse when she checked in. It was the first lie to pass her lips since she was sixteen years old.

This was her fifth day in the small Cornish harbour town but she hadn't unpacked yet.

She wasn't sure she would.

Not now.

Unpacking offered permanency to her visit, a commitment that she would stay.

The man on the beach had changed that with his rasping voice, uneven gait and enquiring eyes.

Julie undid the dressing gown, let it slip from her

shoulders and pulled the T-shirt over her head, careful not to smear the ointment away.

She eyed the mobile phone on the small wooden table beside the bed that served as a nightstand.

Should she call?

The light went out, extinguished in a split second along with the sound of the television.

A muffled curse sounded through the wall, the other guest swearing at a now blank television.

A power cut.

Despite her breath pinching at her lungs, despite her spiked heart rate, Julie had to know.

Was it him?

She reached out her hands in the darkness, cursing when her toe caught the leg of the ancient bedframe and pain radiated through her foot. Limping, she made her way back to the window and ran her thumb down the curtains until she found the edge and peered around the soft fabric.

He wasn't there.

No, wait.

There – next to the plastic waste bin by the wall.

He was drenched now, his hair slicked back and his coat wringing wet while he hunched over and crossed the road.

Coming towards her.

Julie shrank back, trembling, unable to tear her eyes away.

He kept his head down though as if to ward off the deluge assaulting him while he leapt over the gutter and onto the pavement below her window.

She held her breath.

The man paused and reached into his jeans pocket as if he was looking for keys perhaps, and then he took off at a jog.

Her shoulders slumped a little as he disappeared around a kink in the lane.

She exhaled, then dropped her hand from the curtain and blinked as the power flickered back to life.

Her phone emitted a loud *ping*, the chime cutting through the rain hammering against the window as a single line of text appeared on the screen.

Are you OK?

No, she thought. I'm not.

I'm scared.

Chapter Three

When Julie walked downstairs the next morning, a faint light shone through the stained glass insert at the top of the guest house's front door.

The storm had passed, but a vicious wind still beat against the uPVC surface and flapped the letterbox against its brass frame. The steady beat echoed off the narrow hallway walls while she crossed to a spacious dining room at the front of the house.

Patricia, the landlady, was standing at a table in the back corner and talking to a burly man in his late fifties, a copy of a local newspaper open beside him.

'Morning, Julie. Be with you in a minute. Just getting Gerald here sorted out so he can be on his way.'

The man's pale grey eyes shifted away from Julie's scars before a blush crept across his cheeks and then he looked away, rested his arm across the open page and cleared his throat.

'Thanks, Pat. No rush,' she murmured.

She shuffled across to the window, choosing the seat

that faced the way the stranger had walked last night while giving her a clear view of the new guest.

A draught swirled between the ill-fitting sash and after arranging her cutlery the way she wanted it, she gathered her thick woollen cardigan around her waist and peered through the glass.

Where was he?

The net curtain sheltered her from view, pale sunlight reflecting off the ageing polyester, and she shuffled in her seat to stare out across the waves.

The wind sent clouds of sand twirling into the air, scudding across the pebbles and discarded piles of bladderwrack.

Closer to where she sat, at the top of the concrete ramp leading down to the beach, the black council rubbish bin was being shoved inch by inch along the pavement in a battle of wits against the wind.

Julie wondered if it might topple over or be tossed across the street or down the concrete slipway.

She craned her neck to see around the bend in the lane but there was no sign of the man this morning.

Not yet.

'Right, black coffee as usual?'

Julie cried out, her sleeve snagging the knife handle.

It clanged against the side plate, and she reached out to straighten it before looking up at Pat, the woman's face puckered in concern.

'Sorry, love – didn't mean to make you jump.'

'I was miles away there.'

'Hungry?'

Recovering from her fright, Julie took the menu from

her. 'Please could I have two sausages, a poached egg, tomato and toast on the side?'

'Any bacon today? You haven't tried that yet. We get it from a local—'

'No thanks.' She grimaced. 'I don't like the smell.'

'No problem. I'll take this through to the kitchen, and then I'll bring the coffee.'

'Thanks.'

A bergamot aroma drifted towards her while Gerald stirred his tea, the clink of the spoon reminiscent of halyards against masts in the harbour.

She turned back to the window as he flipped to the next page of the newspaper and muttered under his breath.

Eyeing the undulating pebbles beyond the slipway, she wiggled her toes in her battered walking boots and watched while a woman leaned into the wind while she followed a motheaten terrier across the shingle.

The dog paused every few metres, raised its nose and sniffed the air before continuing, his wavering progress and that of his owner driven by whatever scent had caught his imagination.

'Here you go.'

Pat's voice called across from the doorway, and Julie looked over her shoulder as the woman advanced towards her with a steaming plate of food, a cafetiere, and a condiment basket balanced on a plastic tray.

Squeezing out tomato sauce on the side of the plate and adding a liberal sprinkling of black pepper, she heard the man on the other side of the room push his chair back with an exasperated sigh.

He said nothing to his host in farewell and stalked from the room, his brow furrowed.

Julie put down her knife and fork and pushed away the plate, her throat dry as she swallowed the remains of the tomato.

'You look troubled, love.' Pat moved efficiently around the abandoned table, collecting crockery and half-empty jam pots. She placed the newspaper on another table, out of her way while she cleaned.

'He didn't seem very friendly.'

The woman chuckled, placing the tray on the sideboard before returning with a cloth in her hand and wiping down the vinyl tablecloth.

'A busy man, Mr Porter. Visits once a month – I think he must have some sort of consulting job with the harbour. Boats and the like, anyway.'

Julie took a sip of coffee, willing her heart rate to settle. 'Has anyone been asking for me?'

'Not since that phone call three days ago.'

'Okay, thanks.' She turned to the window once more, feigning interest in a crisp packet that tumbled along the kerb beyond the front gate until Pat wandered from the room with the laden tray.

The moment the door swung shut, she scuttled across to the other table, picked up the newspaper and returned to her seat while she turned the pages.

When she'd first walked in, the man – Gerald – had slipped his elbow across the text down on the left-hand side but she had seen the bright coloured advertisement for a local business on the opposite page.

It was on page five.

Just a few lines and a map showing the beaches between here and Plymouth, but enough.

Bad weather curtails Border Patrol efforts.

Exhaling, she ran her eyes down the text, noting an ongoing operation to thwart smuggling activities along the Cornish coastline.

Drugs, contraband cigarettes, alcohol – time had passed, but the old ways stubbornly refused to leave this part of the world.

Folding up the newspaper, Julie stared through the window, seeing nothing while she tried to grasp at a memory that kept sinking out of reach.

Chapter Four

There was a freshness to the air this morning and a bleakness to the washed-out sky when Julie crossed the road to the slipway.

Gulls stalked the pavement, keeping a wary eye on her while she unzipped the canvas satchel slung across her slight frame. They turned away once they realised the plastic container she pulled out was empty.

Her boots were still damp on the uppers from walking the shoreline yesterday, the toes sparkling with dried salt.

Both those and the padded jacket that came down to her knees had been purchased from a local charity shop in a hurry.

The boots pinched her toes and the cuffs didn't quite cover her wrists, but the clothes were serviceable.

Adequate for her needs.

She walked with her head down, searching.

Once a firm believer in turning over every stone to find what she sought, she now took her time, waiting for secrets to reveal themselves.

Some things, some people, didn't want to be found.

It would take time, she reminded herself, and she had plenty of that these days.

Her ankle rolled, her boot sliding over a seaweed-slicked rock, and she threw out her arms to steady herself, heart ratcheting up a notch in fear.

Taking a moment to steady herself, recalling the breathing exercises she'd been taught to calm her nerves, she looked over her shoulder.

A chill caressed her neck despite the thick woollen scarf she wore.

The man from yesterday was only a hundred metres or so behind her but she recognised the uneven gait, the way he kept his weight off his right knee.

A trail of smoke petered out above his bare head, cast away by the stiffening breeze.

Then he raised his hand in greeting.

She waited.

As he drew closer, Julie saw that he hadn't shaved.

A day's growth clung to his jawline and there were dark circles under his eyes that were more visible now than in the gloom of last night's storm.

He dashed the spent cigarette to the ground before shoving his hands in his pockets.

'You shouldn't do that,' she called. 'Those things take decades to decompose.'

'I'll bear that in mind.' He paused a few steps away from her and glared at the churning water. 'I thought the forecast said there'd be an improvement after the storm.'

'More on the way tonight apparently.' Julie inclined

her head towards the slipway, now a good half a mile away. 'Did you have plans?'

He shrugged.

'Sort of. I was expecting someone but I think the storm delayed them.'

'I'd imagine the roads are flooded in places,' Julie said, switching the plastic container to her other hand and shoving her numb fingers into her pocket.

'Maybe that's it.' He forced a smile. 'Did it keep you awake, all that thunder?'

Julie swallowed.

'Only for a while,' she said eventually. 'I think all this fresh air tired me out. I couldn't keep my eyes open. What about you?'

'I couldn't sleep so I went for a walk.'

She turned her attention to the stones and shells once more, chancing a glance from under her overgrown fringe at the dark circles under his eyes and the growth on his jaw.

'Are you staying locally?' she asked casually.

'Close by, yes.'

'In one of the guest houses?'

'No.'

'Oh. Do you have friends here then?'

'None that I know of.' He turned away from her, cupped his hands around another cigarette, the flash of his lighter wavering in the wind before he exhaled the first nicotine-laden smoke skywards and flashed her a smile. 'Do you know anyone down this way?'

'No.'

'Then why did you come here?'

'I needed to get away.'

He chuckled, squinting as he peered out to sea. 'Yeah, that's what I said. You and me – I think we're similar. Both of us running until we couldn't go any further.'

We're nothing alike.

She scowled and turned away, her boots crunching over shingle and broken clam shells, eyes searching.

'What are you looking for today?'

He was following her, his footsteps only a few metres away, his gait as nonchalant as his words.

'Blue sea glass,' she said and kept going.

Another few paces forward, then—

'Why?'

'I'm not sure.' She paused, frowning. 'Actually, I think I do.'

He waited, amusement in his eyes through the pall of smoke before he kicked at a pebble. It scuffed across the sand, a wave covering it within seconds. 'Go on.'

'It's hard to find,' Julie said. 'So it's a challenge, you see. It gives me a purpose.'

'Do you need a purpose?'

'It helps.'

She said nothing more and turned away, leaving him to stare at the waves that lapped at his already sodden shoes.

Chapter Five

Julie was certain now that she'd seen him before.

A lifetime ago.

She perched on the edge of the bed, staring through the window while the stranger hobbled up the slipway from the beach.

She tried to imagine him without the beard, without the worry lines that scored his brow, but her memories pushed back and refused to cooperate.

He leaned against the wall when he reached the road, turning away with a wistful glance towards the broiling sea while he rubbed at his knee.

Evidently walking on the uneven beach aggravated the injury, so why did he do it?

He suddenly straightened, rolled his shoulders and crossed the road below her window, his awkward gait swinging him left and right.

Despite his apparent injury, he walked with purpose, resolve, and Julie wondered what had happened to spur him forward in such a rush before he turned towards the centre of the small town.

Groaning, she lay back and eyed the yellowing swirls of the plasterwork ceiling, an errant cobweb tangled amongst the light fitting swaying in the warmth rising from the radiator under the window sill.

Stay away, they told her to start with.

Then, after eight months, when are you coming back?

That's when she'd fled, packing one suitcase, ignoring the laptop gathering dust on the dining table, and only switching on her phone once a day.

At first, she'd been mortified at the number of missed calls and message notifications that peppered the screen.

Then she simply wondered when they would stop.

Give up hope of ever hearing from her again.

And now…

She ran a hand over her eyes and sat up, then blinked as a familiar figure came into view, his pace frantic.

Gerald hurried along the pavement towards the guest house, his heavy black wool coat open, flapping in the breeze. Face beetroot, his thin hair lifted in wisps as he stumbled up the short path to the front door.

Julie slid from the bed after it slammed shut, shoving her feet into canvas slip-ons and crept to the door.

Heavy footsteps took the stairs, laboured breaths echoing off the narrow landing as Gerald made his way past her room.

She opened the door a crack and heard him grunting under his breath while the sound of hangers slapping against the back of a wooden wardrobe carried to where she stood.

He emerged moments later.

Julie slipped the door back into its frame and held her breath as he walked past.

Stomping back down the stairs, he called out to Pat, then the small brass bell beside the complimentary tourist leaflets rang out.

'Pat? You there?' he called, his voice rasping between gasps.

Julie left her room and eased across the landing to the bannister.

Gerald was standing at the bottom of the stairs, a black canvas holdall at his feet.

He moved from one foot to the other and then spun around as Pat's voice carried from the direction of the kitchen.

'Everything okay?'

'I need to check out early, I'm afraid. There's been a sudden change of plans.'

'I'm sorry to hear that. Is there anything we can do to hel—'

'Just the bill. Thanks.'

'Give me a moment and I'll tot up your account. Will you be paying by card or—'

'Cash. Like last time.'

Julie frowned, sidling across the carpet and hoping the floorboards didn't creak.

Who the hell paid by cash these days?

And why the sudden need to leave?

Had he seen the stranger with the limp?

Did they know each other?

Pat returned, her cheery voice announcing what Gerald

owed, then thanking him profusely at the generous tip he added to the cash he handed over.

'Not at all. I always appreciate your hospitality.'

'I do hope everything is all right though?'

'It is. Nothing to worry about.' His voice petered out as he disappeared from sight, and Julie realised he'd walked into the dining room. 'Have you seen my newspaper?'

'Newspaper?'

'Yes. The one I was reading this morning at breakfast.'

'I haven't I'm afraid. Our cleaning lady's just left for the day. If she put it in the recycling bin, it'll be long gone. The collection was an hour or so ago.'

'Dammit.'

'I'm so sorry. I can phone around and see if anyone has another copy?'

'No, no. There's no time.' He patted his pockets as he returned to the hallway, then pulled out a key fob. 'I need to go.'

With that, he picked up the canvas bag and hurried through the front door, leaving Pat muttering under her breath as she walked back to the kitchen.

Julie raced back to her room and went to the window.

She hadn't driven here, she'd taken the train and then two buses to reach her destination, but there was a small car park behind the terraced houses along the coast path, and she hoped Gerald had used it.

This road was the only way out of town.

She heard it first, then watched as a dark blue hatchback tore past the guesthouse, the driver hunched over the wheel as if trying to make it go faster along the narrow lane.

Automatically, she registered the licence plate, reciting it under her breath as she turned away and sought a pen and paper from her bag.

That done, she eyed the folded newspaper on the dresser, and then picked up her phone, dialling a number from memory.

No one answered.

Cursing, she left a message, her voice clipped while she tried to condense her theory into cohesive instructions.

When she ended the call, she stared at the screen a moment longer.

Would they come?

Would they listen to her, after all this time?

She raised her gaze to the window, to the pebbles and sand, and to the churning waters beyond.

Hope.

There was always hope.

Chapter Six

An agitated surf greeted Julie early the next morning.

Foam and kelp teased against the beach before being torn away once more, the seaweed a reluctant passenger on the retreating waves.

Pushing her unruly hair from her eyes and tugging down her woollen beanie over her ears to combat the wind, Julie's eyes swept the tideline, searching.

A pale pink coloured the sky now, an ominous sign of more unsettled hours ahead if the guesthouse's landlady was to be believed.

Julie didn't trust superstition – she had seen too much in her forty-two years – but she admitted to a sense of foreboding in the salty air as if this place held unfinished business for her.

She shivered and pulled her scarf up to her chin, careful not to snag the fluffy material against her scarred cheek.

Her eyes watered, sand catching on her lashes while she resumed searching the stony sand at her feet.

'Huh.'

Julie crouched, turned over a broken mollusc, then smiled at the bright blue glass that glinted under the weak morning sunlight.

'Found something interesting?'

She spun around, a sickness twisting her stomach as a familiar waft of nicotine blew in her face.

Coughing, she waved her hand in front of her face and blinked.

His head was cocked to one side while he watched her.

Julie held up the shard of blue glass, its edges softened by years tumbling within the sea's clutches.

'You managed to find some. Congratulations.'

'It's rare,' she said. 'These days, anyway.'

'A lucky find then.'

She smiled at his words, despite herself, and peered at the sea wall separating the beach from the coastal road and the tired guesthouses beyond before her eyes found his once again.

'It was, yes.'

'Why is it so rare?'

'They don't use it so much anymore. Everyone uses plastic these days.' A wave ran up the sand, lapping at her toes and she paused to watch the surf churning against the rocks farther along the beach. 'I wonder if it came from a shipwreck…'

'Plenty of wrecks here.' He smiled. 'Including us, right?'

She shivered, turning the blue remnant between her fingers, remembering the sound of glass splintering under intense heat and the burning sensation as splinters tore through her clothing, stabbing her skin.

'Are you all right?'

He reached out his hand, but she stepped away before he could touch her and dropped the sea glass into the plastic container where it landed with a clatter.

When she looked up again, she realised she was farther along the beach than before.

The small fishing village looked too far away, the walls of its horseshoe-shaped harbour a mere speck in the distance.

There was no one else in sight.

'I have to go,' she said. 'I made a mistake coming here on my own.'

'I didn't think to introduce myself properly yesterday.' He took a step closer and put the cigarette between his lips, then wrapped his fingers around her hand before she had a chance to recoil.

'I'm Joe.'

'Julie Nivens. What's your last name?'

'Whitely.' His smile faltered and he held onto her hand a little longer than might have been necessary, then frowned. 'Are you sure I don't know you?'

'We've never met, no.'

'Your name sounds familiar.'

She said nothing, her ears picking out the sound of shoes on gravel, and side-stepped around him, intent on looking at the thin strip of broken shells that washed in with the last wave.

He turned to watch as Julie bent her head to her task,

then cleared his throat and tossed the cigarette stub to one side. 'So, how do you know what to look for, then?'

She couldn't prevent the smile that twitched at her lips, despite the salty air drying her skin, tightening it and sending pinpricks of pain around her jawline.

'I'm good at finding things, I suppose. Especially people.'

Enjoying the confused expression that flashed in his eyes before he took a step away from her, she jerked her chin over his shoulder to the four men who strode towards them, their gait faster now they had found their footing on the uneven surface.

Confusion turned to panic, then panic turned to tired resolution while he watched them.

The taller of the two signalled to the others to fan out while he extracted a pair of handcuffs from his coat pocket, the steel gleaming under the pale light.

Whiteley turned back to Julie, his top lip curling.

'You…'

'Yes, me.'

Julie glared at him, a boldness returning that she hadn't felt in… too long.

'It was me who discovered where you'd been stock-piling your cocaine horde,' she said, her voice stronger now. 'We were searching the warehouse when you decided to firebomb it to try to hide the evidence. You killed a colleague of mine. A good friend.'

'He died while you managed to escape. A ceiling collapsed on top of him,' she added. Her fingertips fluttered to her right cheek. 'It was me who was trapped inside with no way out while the warehouse burned around me.

And it was me who was rescued seconds before the roof caved in.'

A split second later, he was being cuffed by the detective, a man in his late forties who resembled a retired rugby player.

'It was Gerald, wasn't it? I told him he cocked up leaving that newspaper behind. That fucking reporter almost got my name right too,' Whiteley raged, spittle on his lips. 'I told him it was too risky to come here. I told him…'

'Joseph Markus Whiteley, you are under arrest…'

'How did you know I'd come here?' he managed. 'How did you know where to look for me?'

In reply, Julie lifted the plastic container and rattled it under his nose, the blue sea glass jostling for space amongst the tiny shells and stones.

'I told you,' she said. 'I'm good at finding things.'

Lowering her collection of finds before Whiteley was led away by two of the other plain-clothed police officers, Julie turned to the detective at her side.

'Looks like we found you just in time,' he said, his brow knitted together.

'You got my message then?'

'This morning – you were lucky. I wasn't meant to be on call until this afternoon.'

She exhaled, losing some of the tension in her shoulders. 'We got him, Lucas. We finally caught him. Here, of all bloody places.'

'Well, you did say you'd go to the ends of the earth to find him.' He grinned as she reached out to slap his arm.

Rachel Amphlett

His laughter faded, and then his eyes narrowed against the sand being whipped up by the wind.

He reached into his pocket and held out a slim black wallet to her.

'I think this belongs to you.'

When she opened it, tears traced the lines in her scarred cheek, blurring her vision.

A warrant card crinkled under the plastic protective cover, and she sniffed as her thumb traced the familiar creases in the leather.

'I take it that you're ready to come back to work, detective?' said Lucas.

Julie peered along the beach towards the battered guesthouses, the forlorn and shuttered windows staring sightlessly back at her, then turned back to her colleague.

'I am, yes.'

THE END

80

The Man Cave

The Man Cave

Forcing open eyelids crusty with sleep and dried tears, Darren raised his chin and choked back the urge to take a deep breath.

A fetid stink clung to the air, one that suggested whatever that smell was, there were sure as hell particles of it hanging around, waiting to creep across his tongue before seeping into his lungs.

An underlying stench of rotten *something* lingered as an undertone to the overall atmosphere.

Perhaps it was vegetables in the dustbin he could see through the cobweb-cracked window near the ceiling.

Perhaps a leftover chicken carcass.

Perhaps not.

He lowered his gaze, a single tear rolling over his cheek with embarrassment at the stain covering his lap.

His beat-up sneakers had swept scruffy arcs over the debris-strewn and dusty concrete floor, the footprint-shaped grey rainbows a reminder of the hours he'd already spent trying to shuffle out of the hard wooden pine chair he was tied to.

Through the window – a solitary pane maybe eight inches high and a foot wide, and too narrow to squeeze through – weak sunlight teased and danced its way from the horizon.

Shivering, his body craving warmth and clothing more suitable to being held captive than ripped denim jeans and a thin late-eighties Aerosmith T-shirt, he realised the solid weight of his Rolex watch was missing from his wrist.

He gritted his teeth.

On the wall, over to his right, a decades-old central heating system grumbled and shook itself to life, the pipework next to it rattling as it sent warmth up through the ducting system and into the three-bedroom house.

Darren counted the seconds off in his head before the familiar clanging from the air in the system began, and then the pressure reached temperature, pushing warmth into the rooms above.

Morning, then.

Half past six, to be exact.

Plenty of time to plan his revenge.

Whoever had done this, whoever had attacked him, would pay.

It had been nine thirty when the lights had gone out the night before.

Plunged into darkness, he dropped the knife he had been using to gut the trout and clutched at the sides of the kitchen worktop, shocked and disoriented at the sudden transition before glancing at his watch.

The luminous dials had ruined his night vision in the split second it took to register the time.

Stumbling his way past the ceramic sink clogged with grime and gristle, hands held out in front of him, he'd located the keys hanging on an old iron nail next to the back door. He fumbled a cylindrical fob on the ring and twisted it clockwise.

The miniature flashlight was a goofy consolation prize from a fair in Clearfield two years ago when he'd been trying to win a giant teddy bear for Tess. Now the narrow beam provided enough light to guide him to the cellar door.

As he ran his gaze over the fuse box fastened to the wall at the top of the wooden staircase, he'd spotted the trip switch in its off position and reached out to flick it back on.

He frowned while he tried to recall any noise, any warning that preceded the blow to his shoulder that sent him tumbling down the flight, each tread adding bruises to his arms, his legs, his hips.

All he could remember was a blinding flash as the power returned and the lights ignited – and then darkness when the back of his skull met the rough concrete surface of the cellar floor.

Had they tied him up and then ransacked the house, searching for cash, his laptop and more?

Darren clenched his teeth, then ran his tongue over his split lip and squinted as the sun crested the edge of the dusty window sill, ducking his head to the side as a single ray sought him out, blinding him.

Digging his heels into the dust, he heaved the chair

away from the light, groaning under the strain, wishing he had listened to his wife and lost those extra pounds around his waist.

Sweat beading at his brow, panting with the effort, he vowed to get in shape the moment he got home. For now, at least he was out of the sun's glare.

That would have to do.

He peered at the window a moment longer, resigned to the acknowledgement that it was too small for his thickset frame to squeeze through, and then turned his head and ran his gaze over two metal filing cabinets that lined the stone wall of the basement to his left.

A workbench stood beside them, its surface wiped clean and free from dust.

The cabinets had been there when his grandfather had been alive, salvaged from a garage sale a couple of miles away then used to collect mismatched nuts and bolts, torn pieces of worn and scratched sandpaper, a fist-sized ball of rubber bands – the detritus of sixty years of saving bits and pieces.

Just in case.

Darren had found his own use for the cabinets over the years since his grandfather's death. He cleared away the rusting history and spent a whole weekend filling bags he then took to the dump on the outskirts of town before he returned and oiled the locks.

Tess had never liked the house, or its remote and wild location beyond the urban sprawl of the city, and refused to visit after the first time she had set eyes on it. She had begged him to sell it every year of their six-year marriage, telling him it gave her the creeps.

He couldn't.

The place held too many memories, too much history to simply discard it like some unwanted object.

Who knew what would become of the place in his absence if he sold up?

Instead, he returned to the house every two months and chipped away at the jobs that needed doing, organising and cataloguing the history that remained.

A shovel and a pickaxe were propped against the far wall. There were tools in two of the filing cabinet drawers, including pliers and saws.

He knew because he prided himself on keeping them in pristine condition, ready to use at a moment's notice. The rugged terrain around the property was treacherous, with ankle-ripping tree roots entangled around granite rocks and boulders that made it impossible to move fast.

Darren kept a routine – every eight weeks, he would carve his way through the undergrowth, carrying the tools and pushing a wooden barrow that had once been used to transport coal between the outbuilding and the house each winter.

Even the barrow propped next to the back door served a different purpose since his grandfather had passed away.

And now the house had been invaded, his memories soiled by whoever had attacked him last night.

Thank God Tess hated the house.

Thank God she hadn't been here when it happened.

Who knew what could have happened to her otherwise?

The thought of strangers traipsing over the oak floor-boards, wandering through the gnarled woodland surrounding the house tensed his shoulders. A flare of anger replaced confusion, a renewed determination to escape driven by a need for revenge that burned his gut.

There would be something in those drawers he could use to aid his escape, he was sure.

If only he could get into them.

A chink of sunlight caught the locks, polished and gleaming, teasing.

Where were the keys?

They had been in his hand the night before – before he'd been assaulted, before the lights came back on.

Had he clutched them in his hand as he'd fallen, or had he dropped them at the top of the stairs?

Darren craned his neck, rocking the chair back until he could see up the stairs in the gloom.

No keys taunted him from the thirteen treads leading up to the closed cellar door.

He cursed under his breath and let the chair fall forward with a dull thud, his stomach sinking with the realisation that there would be no easy escape.

As if realising his predicament and determined to taunt him, the trill of his mobile phone ringing upstairs filtered down through the closed door to where he sat lashed to the chair.

He recognised the lame tune he'd finally downloaded earlier in the summer, a rock anthem he and Tess had fallen in love with at college.

The sort of song the car radio got turned up for – loud.

The sort of song they sang together, laughing at the memories it evoked.

Tess—

The phone rang out, and he wondered if it had been her trying to reach him.

At least she was safe.

She'd complained about the four-day software conference out of town, saying they could have had a long weekend away together instead if it wasn't for the job promotion she wanted.

He closed his eyes.

Three more days until she returned to their apartment.

Three days until she discovered he hadn't returned from the house in the woods.

His tongue scratched across the roof of his mouth and he blinked, attempting to lose the spots that were forming at the periphery of his vision, blurring the edges of his sight. He crunched his eyelids closed. The headache had started again, wrapping its fingers around the base of his skull before crawling over his head and punching him between the eyes.

A clear plastic bottle of water caught his attention, the bright blue screw-on cap visible above the vice clamped to the edge of the workbench.

He licked his lips and tried to remember when he'd placed it there, whether it was full – and if the bottle was full of water, or turpentine or white spirit instead.

No matter – he couldn't reach it from here, unless…

Darren dug his heels into the floor.

First, he shuffled and scraped until he'd turned the chair – from his attempt to find the keys, he'd deduced it was easier travelling backwards rather than forwards while his calves were tied to the wooden legs.

Next, he shoved the chair towards the workbench.

Dig in, shove.

Dig in, shove.

The scrape of wood against concrete bounced off the cinderblock walls and reverberated in his skull, aggravating the headache, making it worse.

Taking deep gulps of air, panting from the effort, he wondered if anyone had heard him, and held his breath for a moment.

Nothing. Just the buzz of flies and the creaking of the window frame as it expanded in the sun's glare.

Dig in, shove.

Dig in, shove.

Gritting his teeth, he reached the first filing cabinet and turned his head, grimacing as half a dozen flies lifted into the air from the locked drawers and buzzed around his nose and mouth.

He shook his head, growling under his breath, then continued his journey past the second filing cabinet. A bloody fingerprint smudged the top drawer's lock and he wondered fleetingly why he hadn't wiped it away.

He paused to catch his breath.

Tess had been nagging him these past two months to join a gym, but he'd never seen the point. He could lift several pounds, he'd argued. He did so every day in his construction job. Why pay to lift weights during his time off?

Not weights, cardio, Tess had said, her lips pursed – and then she'd shaken her head and walked away.

Now, with sweat beading his brow and neck, dripping between his shoulders, he wondered if he should have listened to her.

He let his head drop forward, the strain in his shoulders burning his muscles while the ropes that bound his wrists behind the chair dug into his skin.

Survival. That's what this was about.

He had to get out of here. Had to find out who had done this.

Dig in, shove.

Dig in, shove.

Now his shoulder was level with the vice clamped to the workbench, the steel surface of the table clear from tools and only an old rag and the water bottle to show for his last venture down here.

Darren jerked his wrists, testing the plastic ties that held him – but they wouldn't yield. Instead, the edges cut into the skin, blood trickling across his palms and over his fingers.

He licked his lips then shuffled closer to the workbench, craning his neck, his mouth apart like a cat fish seeking bait.

Baring his teeth, he lunged for the bottle, biting the blue cap.

It was heavier than he expected. His heart lurched as his mouth took the weight, panic setting in at the thought that it would topple and roll away from him.

He bit down harder and dragged it over the edge of the bench, swiping it away.

The bottle dropped into his lap and rolled forward.

Darren clenched his knees together, tipped the chair back and emitted a cry as the precious water stopped in its tracks.

Lowering his head, he used his teeth to right it between his knees, then paused.

How tight had he screwed the cap back on?

He had a habit of twisting bottle caps tight – and then, as an afterthought, would give it a little extra twist. Paranoia, caused by a bottle of soft drink tipping over in the car one afternoon after a football game and Tess complaining about the sweet stench in the upholstery for weeks afterwards.

His breathing was hollow now, hot and desperate.

Tightening his grip, he chewed the cap between his teeth and twisted.

Nothing – except a dull ache at the base of an incisor that reminded him that his jaw had taken a beating on the way down the cellar steps.

Angrier, in pain, he ran his tongue across his teeth before repositioning them around the bottle cap.

He clenched his thighs, forcing pressure into his knee joints to grip the bottle, and twisted once more.

It happened so fast, it took him a moment for his brain to process what had gone wrong.

The cap loosened from the bottle with little warning, jerking Darren's head backwards.

Shocked by the sudden movement, he relaxed his legs, the dull *squish* of the plastic bottle bouncing off the concrete floor reaching him a split second after he could react.

'No—'

Too late, he shifted in the chair in time to see the bottle roll under the workbench leaving a trail of precious water to mark its trajectory.

Darren let his head drop forwards, closed his eyes, and cursed.

It couldn't be money. He owed no-one anything – he and Tess paid their bills on time, lived a frugal life, and never borrowed, apart from the mortgage on the apartment.

Blackmail?

There hadn't been any threats, no warnings.

Who knew about the house?

There were no signposts to it back on the road, and the undulating track was almost half a mile long, overgrown and unkempt compared to the back of the property. Deliberately so, designed to keep people away when he wasn't around.

That and the chain across the track a few yards before the house came into view.

Movement next to his right foot pulled him from his thoughts, and he glanced down.

No.

No, no, no.

Beady eyes appraised him, nose twitching as the rat raised itself on its hindquarters. Without warning, it scampered across his feet to the water droplets that dotted the floor and began to lap.

Darren lashed out with his foot, a grunt of satisfaction escaping his mouth as the rodent's body landed with a soft thud against the nearest filing cabinet.

It wasn't dead.

The rat glared at him with a disdain that sent a shiver across his shoulders, then raised its nose to the metal drawers, unperturbed by the flies gathering there.

Darren wasted no time. He dug his heels in and made slow, painful progress back to the cellar steps.

The rat watched him for a moment, then began to clean itself, rubbing tiny paws over its whiskers and nose.

Darren kept his eyes on the rodent and craned his neck until he could see the cellar door and called out.

'Is anyone up there? Hello?'

He clamped shut his mouth, his teeth rattling together.

The walls were thick, thicker than they were when his grandfather died. Reinforced. Sound-proofed with the best quality materials he could find.

He had no idea how the rat had got in, and he didn't care.

Darren choked back the next thought that entered his head.

Was his attacker coming back?

What if he had been left here, abandoned?

Forgotten?

What if something had happened to the person who had shoved him down the stairs?

What if no-one else knew he was here?

Tess was away for three more days, and now he had no water. While she was at that software conference, dining out in five star luxury morning and night, he was here.

Trapped.

Sure, he reckoned he could last without food – but water?

The rat lowered its paws and eyed him, a raw hunger in its eyes.

He smacked dry lips, tried to batten down the panic, and failed.

'Help me!'

The words were out of his mouth before he could stop them. He clamped his mouth shut, shocked by the fear trembling his voice.

Then—

A footfall, above his head as if someone had stepped into the kitchen and paused.

'Hello? Who's there?'

The seconds passed, the silence drawing out until he couldn't bear it any longer.

'Let me out!'

'How are you doing down there, Darren?'

'Tess?' Utter confusion clutched at his chest. 'Is that you?'

'Did you have a busy weekend planned?'

His brow creased, his thoughts spinning. 'I thought you were away. I thought you weren't coming back until Monday.'

A sigh carried through the door.

A sigh that held pain, loathing, disgust.

'I know about the others, Darren.'

Her voice was soft, musical.

That made the accusation even worse.

'What others? I've never cheated on you, Tess. That's the truth.'

She didn't answer right away, and his breath caught in his throat.

He'd been so careful. All this time, he'd been so careful…

'Let me tell you what I know, Darren. The first filing cabinet is for purses, watches and cell phones…'

Rachel Amphlett

Gritting his teeth, he strained at the plastic ties cutting into his flesh.

How could she know?

How did she find out?

'The second filing cabinet...' Her voice broke, then there was a loud sob before she beat the cellar door with her fist. 'How could you?'

He glared across the basement at it now, the flies buzzing at the drawers, headbutting the cool steel surface in vain, the inquisitive rat sniffing at the metal surfaces, seeking a way in.

'That's where you keep everything else, isn't it Darren?'

Yes, the voice in his head screamed.

Everything else.

Everything catalogued.

Everything organised.

'Fingers, Darren,' Tess said, her voice little more than a whisper.

He could sense her, trembling at the door while she spoke the words to him, her mouth close to the thick oak surface.

'Lips,' she said. 'Toes... The rest... I found the graves out in the woods, Darren.'

'Wait, Tess. You don't understand. Don't call the police.'

She laughed then, a rich guttural burst that exuded bitterness – and something else.

He reared back in shock, the chair tilting on its legs. 'Tess?'

'I'm the only one who knows you're here,' she said, a

96

menace creeping into her voice, a bitter confidence he hadn't heard before. 'No-one knows about the house except me, do they?'

'No…'

It was true. He never invited anyone here. Never mixed with the locals. Kept his distance.

For good reason.

'The police aren't coming,' she hissed. '*No one's* coming. You can rot down there, Darren Forbes. You deserve to die a slow death for what you've done.'

She thumped the door once before her footsteps retreated from the top of the stairs.

He peered up at the ceiling as she paced across the kitchen, her heels clacking on the wooden floorboards, and then the back door slammed shut.

A car engine roared to life beyond the grimy window before he heard the wheels crackle across the stony ground.

'Tess?'

His gaze dropped from the window to the filing cabinets, to the flies buzzing around the drawers.

He heard their tiny wings beating, heard the scratching and scurrying beside the workbench as the rodent became inquisitive once more, and then its nose appeared, twitching as it sought him out.

Darren threw back his head and screamed.

'Tess!'

THE END

A Dirty Business

A Dirty Business

Michael Hawkins pulled a well-worn pair of soft leather gloves over his calloused hands and tugged a woollen beanie over his ears.

Condensation escaped his chapped lips in a fine mist while he locked his vehicle, a trickle of fine water droplets coating the hood of the years-old 4x4 where only half an hour ago a thick layer of frost had covered the metalwork.

The drive to the recycling centre wasn't long – only twenty minutes from home – and his fingers were still numb from scraping clean the windshield while the engine idled. The heater had finally kicked in as he'd swiped his security card at the gates into the facility, wafting a token gust of warm air across his steel-toed safety boots before he'd turned the key in the ignition and reluctantly climbed out.

Two years, three months and two days.

That was how long he'd been sorting people's trash.

Despite the fresh pair of overalls and work shirt he

wore underneath his thick fleece and hi-vis vest, he already felt dirty just looking at the damn place.

He clutched a stainless steel coffee cup in his left hand and raised it in greeting to Brian Lockie as he trudged towards him, forcing a smile while the older man paused to unlock the dilapidated trailer they shared as an office this side of the site.

Overhead, gulls wheeled and dived above the landfill pits, eager to discover what morsels remained after the previous day's recycling and trash collections while a backhoe worked amongst the plastic and twisted metal-work, its engine rumbling across to where he stood.

Michael wrinkled his nose while Brian entered the office.

After two days off – Lisa thought he was at a training conference – the stench from the place took some getting used to.

When he first started the job, she made him leave his boots on the porch before walking into the house, and even then he had to take a shower downstairs before she let him enter the kitchen or den.

She hadn't even done that when he'd spent four horrific weeks sweeping the floor at the local slaughter-house before he quit, unable to stomach the surroundings.

Now he kept a change of clothes in the downstairs bathroom and a separate laundry basket for his work over-alls, just to keep her happy.

It was easier when they were first married.

Keeping her happy.

He sniffed – not too hard – then took a sip from the travel cup, savouring the bitterness.

Brian peered around the office door, his expression perplexed. 'Were you here earlier?'

'No, sir. Half seven is early enough for me.' Michael paused on the threshold as his colleague turned and pointed at the computer screen under a single window overlooking the parking lot. 'Why?'

'The system says you clocked in twenty minutes ago.'

'Huh.' He reached into his fleece pocket and withdrew his security card. 'Well, this has been in my jacket pocket since last night. I always put it there so I don't forget.'

'What about your spare?'

Each of them carried a master key card in case of emergencies. It was why they earned a meagre amount more than their junior colleagues, and why they took it in turns to be on call-out.

'At home. I keep it in the top drawer of my nightstand.'

Brian frowned, weathered skin creasing his brow. 'The system must be faulty, then. I'll give head office a call. I need to chase them up about getting the CCTV installed anyway.'

'We're due to open in ten.' Michael checked his watch. 'While you're doing that, I'll check the containers are ready.'

'Okay. Call me on the radio when we're good to go.'

Michael caught the walkie-talkie Brian tossed to him, held it up in salute and turned away.

An articulated truck carrying a full load from the previous day's recycling efforts roared past the office trailer, the building rocking gently in its wake, and Michael paused at the door while the driver maneuvered through the wide steel exit gates until it was safe for him to cross to the enormous corrugated iron bins that lined a horseshoe-shaped concrete pit.

Approaching a set of concrete steps to the right of the pit, he cast his gaze over lines of washing machines and driers that formed a forlorn white- and stainless-steel honor guard each side of him.

Beyond those, ovens and cookers peeked out between the gaps as if searching for a way to escape before being stripped of all recyclable parts, their remains then crushed beyond recognition.

An impatient honk reached his ears when he rested his hand on the metal handrail of the stairs leading up to the pedestrian access points, and he emitted a mirthless chuckle under his breath.

There was always one.

The recycling centre opened at eight o'clock sharp – not a minute earlier, and not a minute later.

Until Brian released the automatic locks on the gates, not one car would be passing through them.

Climbing the steps, Michael ran his gaze over the twelve metal bins that were set down ready for the first wave of recycling.

Each bin was positioned beneath a signpost bolted to a metal barrier that prevented members of the public from toppling in while they deposited their trash.

Each signpost denoted the intended contents of the bin – cardboard, metal, electronics, garden waste.

In front of those, a row of parking spots were painted onto the raised concrete pier that curved around the facility so that the public could park and empty their vehicles.

A pair of ravens – or were they crows? He could never remember – pecked and squabbled over a greasy grey scrap of meat they'd found at the top of the concrete steps, the sinew stretching between beak and claw as they tore it to pieces and bickered.

They squawked in disgust when he clapped his gloved hands together, flapping their way into the air before landing amongst the stark branches of a withered hornbeam behind four blue clothing bins, the bright paintwork hurting his eyes.

He shouldn't have, but when Heather phoned him on his way home on Tuesday night and suggested sneaking away from Lisa for a couple of nights, he couldn't resist.

Lisa and he were arguing more than ever, and the lie came easily.

After all, he and Brian often attended health and safety courses in Newark – it was the closest place the waste and recycling company offered training – and Lisa wasn't to know he was due a couple days off in lieu of overtime, was she?

Now the lack of sleep – and the activities that prevented him from sleeping – was taking its toll.

He took another sip of coffee, willing the caffeine to kick in.

Ten years ago, he would've shrugged off the tiredness and got on with it. Forty-five and – if he were honest – carrying a little extra weight around his middle, he wondered for a fleeting moment what the hell he was playing at.

The pang of guilt faded the moment he recalled Lisa

nagging him to deal with the trash on his way out the door that morning.

That had started the next argument.

The previous one had started when he'd walked in at half ten the night before, after the 'conference' had ended.

He ended up sleeping on the sofa, which didn't help the ache in the small of his back.

Then, an hour ago, Lisa had thrown up her hands in disgust and stormed out the front door, saying she had better things to do than clear up after him and that he should know better, given his job.

She was still muttering under her breath as she fired up the ancient red sports car she refused to sell and reversed out of the driveway, the wheels spinning across ice-covered asphalt as she tried to floor it down the street.

The trash remained outside the back door.

Michael sighed and trudged towards bin number twelve, the nearest to him.

Signposted 'metals', within the hour it would be full to the brim with discarded cheap watches, costume jewelery, unwanted gardening tools, and more.

However, safety precautions dictated that before any members of the public were permitted into the site, each bin had to be checked in case of any problems that might cause a health concern.

Resting a hand on the metal railing, feeling the cold seeping through his gloves, Michael leaned over the precipice and peered into the container.

All clear…

He was turning away when something glistened in the bright cold sunlight.

He froze.

A slender sports wristwatch lay in the far corner, its face turned upwards and the grey-coloured strap curled underneath.

He paused and leaned closer, squinting.

'Huh.'

It looked similar to the one Heather wore, and he wondered how much she'd paid for hers.

She wore it everywhere, even when she wasn't planning to go for a run, just so she could count her daily steps.

Would it be worth salvaging?

Maybe he could get something for it if he sold it online…

Another honk from the waiting line of cars pulled him from his thoughts, and he turned away from the railing, resigned.

Chances were, it was a cheap imitation, which was why it had been thrown away.

It must've got caught on something, which was why it hadn't fallen out with the rest of the trash when the container had been emptied at the end of the previous day's shift.

He'd have a word with Brian about the person responsible for hosing out the bin afterwards, though.

He shook his head and scuffed across the concrete pier to bin number eleven.

Electronic goods.

Cell phones, Bluetooth speakers, discarded car sat nav systems – it all ended up in here.

It never ceased to amaze him how quickly bin eleven filled over the course of any given day.

He still used the phone he was given when he worked for a telecoms company – until they downsized after *that* particular year and he found himself surplus to requirements – and it worked just fine, even if there was a hairline fracture in the bottom right hand corner of the screen.

He wouldn't – couldn't – contemplate throwing it away and buying a new one, not the way the bills were stacking up on the kitchen table back home.

The steel-capped toe of his boot caught against the empty container as he swept his gaze across its floor, the solid *clang* echoing off the sides.

His heart skipped a beat – painfully – and when he swallowed, his tongue rasped within a dry mouth.

A single sleek cell phone lay in the middle of the container, its screen visible, all the little icons littering the display as its power flickered and threatened to fade.

A shiver crinkled its way down Michael's spine.

There was the luminescent pink square of the banking app Heather favoured.

Above it, the bright green of the encrypted messaging app they favoured so that Lisa wouldn't find out about their affair or their secret meetings while she was at work in that beauty parlor she co-managed Monday through Friday.

He gripped the railing with both hands, his thoughts tumbling over one another.

What was going on?

Lifting his gaze to the remaining bins, he thought he heard a car engine purring beyond bin number three, but his view was blocked by another row of bell-shaped bins used for collecting glass bottles.

He sniffed the air, catching a whiff of exhaust fumes, then glanced over his shoulder.

The gates were still closed, and now Brian was standing at the mobile office door, watching him.

The radio in his pocket crackled to life.

'I'm waiting to open the gates. Everything all right up there?'

Michael fished out the walkie-talkie. 'I think so.'

Even he heard the tremor in his voice.

'What's going on?' Brian barked. 'I've got cars backed up as far as the junction down here.'

'Won't be a minute.'

He shoved the radio back in his pocket and jogged around the lip of the bin to the next one.

Number ten.

Shoes.

Taking a deep breath, he peered in.

A single tan stiletto lay in the left-hand corner below his position.

Three-inch heel, slightly worn down on the outer edge, and…

'Size four,' he murmured.

He reached up and ran a gloved finger under his collar, sweating now despite the chill breeze that whipped across the concourse below and up to where he stood, making his eyes water.

His stomach lurched, and he turned, grasping hold of the railings as he gulped deep breaths and tried to steady his rising heartbeat.

Then his gaze traveled to the blue clothing bins lined

up on the other side of the parking bays and he cried out in shock.

A bright pink sweatshirt now curled out from the letter-box-shaped hole in the bin on the far left, a dark stain covering the sleeve.

His radio squawked again, but he didn't hear Brian's words, and took no notice of the man's obvious irritation at his lack of response either.

Instead, Michael's attention was taken by movement at the far end of the line of corrugated containers.

To the battered red sports car that belched exhaust fumes in a blue fog that swirled across the icy concrete pier.

To the woman whose shoulder-length hair was captured underneath a woollen beanie that he'd given her last winter, a satisfied smile on her lips.

To the woman standing beside bin number three.

'Organic waste'.

He spun around at the sound of running footsteps to see Brian heading towards him, his cheeks flushed with the effort, his expression furious, and held up his hand before he could get any closer.

'Call the cops, Brian.'

His colleague slowed to a walk, confusion creasing his brow. 'What?'

'Call the police. Now!'

He didn't hear Brian's response.

Instead, Michael ran towards the car, towards Lisa as she reached out and popped open the trunk, sliding to a halt on a patch of ice, his arms wheeling about his head as he tried to find his balance.

She was opening the trunk now, her movements unhurried while his breath escaped in short, panicked bursts.

'Lisa? Lisa – what're you doing?'

She turned, blood stains on her jeans and a calculated expression in her eyes.

His spare security pass dangled from a lanyard around her neck, and her sleeves were rolled up to her elbows, business-like.

He peered behind her, bile rising in his throat at the pale arm that snaked out from under the old dog blanket, the one he kept folded up on top of the workbench in the garage, the one she was always nagging him to throw away ever since their spaniel had died a year ago.

'What have you done, Lisa?' he repeated, a cold chill snaking around the back of his neck. 'What have you done?'

She moved to one side so he could see the crumpled form she'd crammed into the trunk, Heather's blank eyes staring up at him.

'I'm doing what I asked you to do this morning,' Lisa said, brushing a strand of dark brown hair from her eyes with the back of her hand. 'I'm taking out the trash.'

THE END

THE END

The Last Super

Chapter One

Seventeen years, nine months and four days.

And it would all be over within the next five hours.

Larry Patrick raised his chin, straightened his tie, then patted his pockets.

Wallet, keys, cellphone.

He ran his eyes over the cardboard cartons lining the living room wall, taped shut and ready to go. Books, some vinyl records – Lou Reed, Pink Floyd, all the good stuff from the seventies – crockery and clothes.

Dust motes floated in the air and caught the morning sunlight that always struck the front window – never enough to warm the ground-floor apartment, but sufficient to provide a hint of the temperature outside.

The new RV Carol and Gary Petersen had bought with their share of the developer's settlement stood was parked out front.

Thirty-three feet long, sleek, modern.

It took Gary four attempts to shuffle the monstrosity into a tight space between an ancient blue Civic and a

Korean-made coupé Larry didn't know the name of, with Carol's attempts to guide her husband not boding well for their impending trip to Florida.

Any other time, there would have been an uproar out there. Someone would complain that it was blocking their view.

Except that the brownstones over the road were boarded up, abandoned these past three weeks.

Even the one painted a peachy hue that always reminded him of the desert at sunset.

An array of trash fluttered against its front stoop as if trying to climb up and seek out a new home beyond the peeling paintwork of the front door, the one with a new padlock fitted to its rusting handle.

Larry lowered his gaze and wondered if he should change out of his monogrammed shirt and into something more casual.

It wasn't as if he would be the building supervisor for much longer.

He huffed under his breath, straightened his shoulders.

No, he would wear it. After all, he still had a job to do, didn't he?

Even if it was only for the next five hours.

Back in 2001, it was all the work he could get.

Too old to go and fight again.

Too young to retire.

Until now.

Rebecca, his daughter, had persuaded him to move closer to her and her husband. A new condo development in Virginia Beach, only a mile or so from where they lived with his two grandkids.

He frowned as he ran his thumb over a piece of tape on one of the cartons, ironing out the creases.

As soon as Bec and David heard the final contracts were signed on the redevelopment, they insisted he move away from the city and, despite the payout he got from the developers, he couldn't afford Virginia Beach on his own.

He argued with them for a time.

He didn't win.

His daughter pointed out that since her mom had walked out on them both eighteen years ago, she owed him.

For the food he put on the table every night.

For the education that got her through college and into university.

For everything.

Now, she was paying him back.

It was because of their idea, their offer of kindness to pay the difference that David was turning up tomorrow with the U-Haul truck to drive him down the coast as the developers began to rip apart his home.

Larry exhaled and moved to the door, his hand shaking as he reached for the handle.

How was he going to tell them that he couldn't leave Baltimore?

Chapter Two

Out in the hallway, his stomach growled as charcoal smoke wafted in through the back door, the promise of grilled steak and a cold light beer tempered with the realization this would be the last time.

The last time they all met up like this to share a meal, catch up with the news, check in on each other.

Would the tenants of the newly refurbished apartments do this in eight months' time when the project was finished?

He wouldn't bet on it.

'Larry!'

He turned at the sound of a cigarette-damaged croak that barked off the walls.

Brenda Friedman, seventy years old – plus a half-decade more by his reckoning – beckoned to him, then handed him a plate of bread rolls and winked.

'Make yourself useful. One each for everyone to start with, plus a burger. There's relish on the table out there, and paper napkins if anyone wants them.'

'Yes, ma'am.' He turned at the sound of an indignant meow to see a large tabby cat peering out from behind the wire mesh door of a kitty carrier. 'You've already packed him?'

'Cats,' said Brenda, and shrugged. 'You know what they're like. They pick up on everything. He'll run and hide if I don't make sure he's somewhere safe.'

'True.' He lowered his voice. 'Any news?'

She shrugged. 'Not a peep. Tried his email last week – that came back undelivered, just like the letter I mailed him three weeks ago.'

'What about that phone number you had for him?'

'I keep leaving messages, but he doesn't call.' She sighed. 'Maybe he just doesn't want to talk to me.'

'Joshua's your son, Brenda.' He reached out and squeezed her arm. 'I'm sure he will, eventually. Don't give up on him.'

'He did time in prison for armed robbery, Larry. I'm the only one who hasn't given up on him.' She patted his hand. 'Don't forget to come get the fruit punch when you're done with the bread.'

Chapter Three

'Hey, Supe.'

Larry paused at the top of the four stone steps to the yard where his neighbors gathered on an uneven patio and grinned as Scott Bancroft raised a bottle of beer in his direction.

'Got you one of these – where've you been?'

'Just checking on a few things.' Careful he didn't trip over one of the cracked and uneven pavers, he crossed to where two trestles had been set out with tablecloths that flapped in a gentle breeze and put the plate of bread rolls beside the relish. 'Water, gas, that sort of thing.'

'It's your last day – take a minute to relax.' Melissa Bancroft called from where she stood beside the smoking grill with a set of tongs in one hand and a glass of iced tea in the other, skin-tight jeans leading up to a Lycra top that clung in all the right places.

Larry smiled. 'Make sure you rehydrate plenty – Brenda's made fruit punch.'

'Thanks for the warning.' Scott handed him the beer, then turned to watch as two kids screamed with laughter. 'Thanks for sorting out the slip 'n' slide for the grandkids, too.'

'That was Brenda. Said we couldn't have a summer cookout without one.'

'She's right about that. At least it'll keep 'em occupied for a while.'

'When is your son getting here?'

Scott grimaced. 'Later, he says. A last-minute meeting with the divorce lawyer.'

'Sorry to hear that.'

'It's his own fault. Wait until you meet his girlfriend.'

Melissa handed the tongs to Gary Petersen and wandered over. 'Larry, in case we don't get the chance later Scott and I wanted to thank you for everything you've done for us over the years.'

He could feel the heat flushing up across his neck towards his jaw and cleared this throat. 'Only doing my job, ma'am. That's all anyone would do in the same position.'

A heavy hand on his shoulder sent a shudder through his spine.

'Don't be so humble,' said Scott, and handed him an envelope. He shrugged, a ripple of muscles flowing across his broad arms. 'A gift, from us. Open it later if you like.'

'You've worked all hours,' added Melissa. 'Every day. We've been here twelve years, Larry and you've always been there for us – and our kids, when they were home.'

He blinked, took the envelope.

Felt the notes inside.

Folded it and shoved it in his back pocket.

'Thank you,' he murmured.

Another slap on the shoulder.

'Larry – fruit punch!'

'I'd best go get that.'

Chapter Four

'It feels strange, doing this on a Thursday.'

Carol sat on the bottom step, smiling at a peal of laughter as her granddaughter shot along the slip 'n' slide. 'Instead of our usual Friday, I mean.'

'I don't think it'd be a good idea to try and have a cookout while the place is being torn apart tomorrow,' said Melissa, her words slurring from the potent cocktail in her hand. 'Dust in the food, for starters.'

They sat around the table under a lone silver maple, the roar and crunch of construction work in the next block over echoing across the rooftops.

Larry said nothing, leaned forward and fanned a napkin over the remains of the salad, dispersing the flies that gathered near a pool of olive oil dressing.

'Mom, maybe you should have a glass of water.'

Stuart Bancroft scowled, his expensive suit crumpled as he passed a paper plate laden with food to the skinny brunette twenty-something who hovered at his elbow.

Larry had already forgotten her name.

'I'm fine,' Melissa gurgled. 'Besides, it's our last time here. Lemme enjoy myself.'

The twenty-something blushed and turned away from her boyfriend and his mother, wandering toward the two kids while she picked at her food.

'Always thought they'd carry me out of here in a box,' said Larry, suppressing a belch as he leaned back in his camp chair. 'Didn't expect to have to move at my age.'

'Me either,' said Brenda, then screeched as a spray of cold water hit them.

'Richie, no!'

Stuart shot off toward the kids, snatched the hosepipe from his son and switched off the faucet as both children burst into tears.

'Oh, my.' Brenda took the towel Carol handed over and wiped at the back of her neck. 'It's all right – it doesn't matter. He didn't mean it.'

'I'm so sorry.' Stuart returned to the table, his face puce. 'It's the divorce. They used to be better behaved.'

Larry took the towel and dabbed at his face. 'No harm meant, I'm sure.'

'Mom – we need to make a move. Sorry, but the babysitter's got a date tonight and we're already running late.'

Melissa raised her hands and sighed. 'Looks like the party's over, folks.'

Chapter Five

The departure of the Bancrofts with their son and grandkids broke up the party, as Melissa predicted.

After tidying away the grill – it was headed to Virginia with Larry – and fetching the last of their belongings from their apartment on the second floor, Carol and Gary climbed into their RV.

'I didn't realize you were leaving tonight as well,' said Brenda, dabbing a tissue to her eyes.

'It's why Gary didn't drink much,' Carol hiccupped.

Her husband smiled, leaning his elbow out of the window and starting to looking comfortable behind the wheel. 'Figured we'd miss some of the traffic – Fridays can be hell on the 95.'

'It's always hell on the 95,' said Larry. He held up his hand. 'Safe travels.'

'Get yourself on social media,' said Carol. 'We'll be sharing the trip as we go.'

'I'll think about it.'

He wandered into the road as Gary started the engine, a

Rachel Amphlett

soft roar emanating from the engine while he waved them out from the tight space, ignoring the frustrated glare from a delivery driver.

Moments later, they were off, hands waving out the windows as the RV purred away, and Larry returned to the curb outside the brownstone.

'I give them six weeks.'

He smiled as Brenda coughed out a snort, her gaze on the departing vehicle.

'Maybe four,' she said.

'You never know, might be what they needed.'

She laughed as a car pulled into the free space and waved to the driver. 'That's my friend, Dorothy. She lives at the retirement place.'

'That's good to have someone you know there to help you get settled. I'll fetch your bags. When are your cartons being collected?'

'Tomorrow, at eight. I spoke to a woman at the developer's office this morning and she's going to come down here and make sure everything's okay.' Brenda narrowed her eyes. 'Wouldn't want anything stolen.'

'Good thinking. I'll keep an eye on them until then.'

Larry hefted the two large suitcases into the back of the compact, placed the kitty carrier on the rear seat and wrapped the seat belt around it.

The cat mewed at him through the wire door, its eyes wide in confusion.

'Don't worry – I'll put butter on his paws,' said Brenda. 'He'll be fine.'

'I'm sure he will.' Larry shut the door, then helped her round to the passenger side as her friend climbed

126

back behind the wheel. 'You behave yourself, Mrs Friedman. Don't start a riot the minute you get there, you hear me?'

'They have poker games on Friday nights,' she said, her eyes sparkling.

'You'll whip the lot of 'em.' He smiled. 'I'm sure your son will be in touch, too. In his own time. I guess he has a lot of things to process at the moment, having his freedom again after fifteen years.'

She paused, her hand on top of the door. 'I'm going to miss you, Larry.'

'Just doing my job, Mrs Friedman.'

She leaned over and kissed his cheek. 'You've been a good friend. Thank you.'

He waved until Dorothy's car disappeared from sight, then wandered up the four steps to the front door, closing it behind him.

The late summer sun cast a glow across the floorboards, the surface pitted and pockmarked from centuries of foot traffic.

He peered up the staircase.

Instead of voices, music and laughter, the building was silent, dead, except for the sound of his own breathing, his heartbeat in his ears as his gaze fell to the door leading down to the basement.

He blinked, attempting to lose some of the lightheadedness from the beer and Brenda's fruit punch and rummaged in his pocket for his keys.

Unlocking the door, he flipped on the light switch and edged down the stone staircase, careful to keep his hand on the plaster wall.

There was no railing, no way to stop his fall if he slipped.

He shivered when he reached the bottom of the stairs and stared at the large furnace in the far corner, its huge frame silent and sulking.

He would miss waking to the noise of the heating system coming to life. Six o'clock, every morning without fail in time for his neighbors – his friends – to have hot water and warmth.

Above his head, pipework crisscrossed the low ceiling under his apartment.

It was why he suggested the basement in the first place.

No-one else came down here but the building supervisor.

No-one else would hear.

Larry's gaze roamed to a patch of pale-colored concrete in the floor, uneven with a rough finish, about five feet by two.

Back-breaking work.

When Brenda's son Joshua hammered on his door all those years ago, he knew something was wrong the minute he'd seen the teenager's face.

He wondered, later, whether Joshua inherited his vicious streak from his father but that night...

That night, none of it mattered.

That night, Joshua decided enough was enough.

Old man Friedman used to beat Brenda so hard she wouldn't be seen for days – and she still had bruises when she emerged from the apartment, skittish as a mouse.

She refused to report him, and back then there wasn't much support for victims of domestic violence.

Joshua waited until his mother had locked herself in the bathroom after another attack, then turned on his dad.

Blind rage turned to panic.

Rebecca was only seven at the time and staying with her paternal grandparents in Brooklyn for the weekend, so she never knew.

Never knew that her father had listened to Joshua's gasping explanation, crossed the hallway and helped the teenager drag his father's body down the basement stairs before his mother realized what happened.

When Brenda emerged from the bathroom an hour later, Joshua said he had told his father to leave, and that he would take care of her.

Which went fine until Joshua killed another man in an armed robbery two years later.

Larry circled the pale concrete rectangle, sweat patches under his arms.

They spent two days chipping away at the floor, away from prying eyes and ears while the neighbors were at work.

On day three, Joshua shoved his father's body into the shallow cavity.

On day four, Larry mixed concrete.

Now the place was going to be redeveloped.

Stripped apart, piece by piece, including the basement.

Where old Harry Friedman lay rotting.

Larry wandered back up the stairs, his tread as heavy as the thoughts that tumbled over in his mind.

Reaching his apartment, he rummaged through one of

the boxes before pulling out a half-full bottle of Jameson's and a tumbler, pouring a generous measure with shaking hands.

He moved to the window, took a sip.

Fished out his cellphone.

Stared at the screen.

If Joshua went back to prison before Brenda got the chance to see him again, it would kill her, of that he was sure. There would be no early release for good behavior like last time, no hope of parole – not within Brenda's lifetime.

He topped up the whiskey, squared his shoulders then dialed 911, clearing his throat as the operator answered.

'I'd like to report a homicide. I killed a man.'

Ending the call a few seconds later, Larry turned the tumbler of whiskey in his hand and raised a silent toast to the empty street beyond the window.

Seventeen years, nine months and four days.

He might be the last super, but he looked after his tenants.

THE END

Something in the Air

Chapter One

The passengers for flight Z341 shuffled weary feet across the baking concrete apron leading away from the departure lounge, the air ominous with the stench of ozone and aviation fuel.

Latecomers staggered as they left the cool air-conditioned terminal, assaulted by an unforgiving environment thick with humidity and the roar of aircraft engines.

In the distance, beyond the flat airfield, away from the straggly eucalypt and palm trees that flanked the chain link security fence, a lightning storm flashed and wavered across the fringes of the hinterland.

Most of the passengers carried hand luggage – a backpack, a laptop case, a roll-along suitcase that would be squashed and coerced into the overhead lockers.

Their faces were a mixture of reluctance and resolve, excitement and trepidation depending on whether their destination was the exhausted end of a trip or the start of something new.

The line shuffled forward, urgent now, eager to get

away following a forty-minute delay after thunder shook the departure lounge glass and rumbled across Queensland's Sunshine Coast while streaks of lightning scorched the clouds.

Amy gripped the nylon strap of her black backpack, knuckles white.

It had been passed through the security checks before she'd arrived at the airport, then thrust at her in a corner of the departure lounge, away from prying eyes.

Jaw clenched, she stepped sideways from the crocodile line obediently following the zig-zagging yellow lines towards the aircraft.

She watched as a man in a black suit jacket and jeans stared sightlessly from his perch near the top of the steps, his eyes obscured behind sunglasses, his mouth downturned as an indignant screech pierced the humidity.

She shifted her gaze to a man and child approaching the steel steps leading up to the fuselage.

The toddler was loud and insistent, snatching away her hand from her father's and stretching out to reach up to the rail. The little girl shook her head when the man offered assistance, his arm hovering above her slender shoulders, his face lined with worry.

In front of them, already climbing the steps, was a steady stream of men and women gazing across at the waiting line below with a degree of smugness.

'He should pick her up.'

Amy glanced over her shoulder to see a woman in her mid-sixties glaring at the steps, then turned back and hurried to keep up with the queue, eyeing the boarding pass in her hand.

Seat C3.

Business class.

Near the front, an aisle seat.

Despite what the boarding pass said, despite any hope she would be seated before everyone else, the passengers were being boarded at the same time in an attempt to get the plane off the ground without further delay.

Another five minutes shuffling forward in the queue, and then Amy climbed the steel staircase – careful not to leave her fingerprints on the rail – and entered the gloom of the cabin, goosebumps sweeping across her bare arms while she blinked to adjust her vision.

She frowned, recalling the seat map that was shown to her at the last minute.

Only one passenger beside her, in seat A.

D and F were on the other side of the cabin.

No B, no E, not until you passed beyond the thick soundproof flame retardant curtains and into the economy cabin.

Just under two hundred seats in total. And almost all of them were full this morning.

All adults, apart from the one little girl farther along in economy, eyes wide with anticipation while her seatbelt was fastened around her.

Amy swallowed.

How many innocent people could be injured or worse by her actions?

Bystanders, the journalists would call them when it was all over.

Collateral damage, said the man who disappeared into the crowded terminal after handing her the bag.

She had lost sight of him within seconds.

'Good morning.' The female flight attendant beamed, flashing perfect teeth amongst impeccable make-up.

Amy forced a smile, handed over her boarding pass even though she could see her allotted place waiting for her, teasing her with its proximity.

Sarah, the woman's name tag pronounced, the brass effect catching in the overhead lights and making Amy blink as she took back the pass.

The same woman who had been working at the departure gate moments before.

The same woman who had allocated her the seat, lips pursed at the last-minute change, eyes worried.

No matter now.

It was too late to turn back.

Turning away, Amy swung her bag from her shoulder and hurried to take her place.

The man in the business jacket and jeans glanced up at her as she approached, his sunglasses perched on top of his head now, green eyes darting to the exit door as she lowered herself into her seat beside him.

He was pale, any semblance of a tan fading beneath the collar of his white shirt while he ran a finger underneath it, blanching as the final passengers boarded.

She ignored him and instead placed her bag under the seat in front of her where she could see it before arranging her long legs and tucking her flowery long skirt around her ankles and fastening her seatbelt.

As she clipped the buckle into place, she spotted her neighbour's boarding card sticking out from the seat pocket in front of him.

Jed McIntyre.

Then a man's overstuffed carry-on bag scraped her bare shoulder, and she grimaced, flicking her hand while he apologised before hurrying away.

'You'd have thought he'd have put that in the hold,' murmured the man beside her, his voice unsteady.

'Too much hassle to wait for it at the other end, I suppose. Cairns can be busy at the best of times,' she replied, before eyeing an identical backpack to hers squeezed between his feet. 'Travelling light?'

'This time.' He cleared his throat. 'A last minute trip. You?'

'Something like that.'

Chapter Two

The steady drone of the aircraft's twin engines coalesced with the murmur of passengers' voices as it climbed steadily away from the coast to find its route north.

They had left the storm behind, reaching a cruising altitude of thirty-five thousand feet in a steady banking motion before levelling out.

Amy listened to the regular pings and announcements, the final one a warning to remain seated in case of turbulence as her ears popped with the changing cabin pressure.

Gaps within a soft carpet of tumbling grey and white clouds revealed glimpses of a turquoise coast giving way to darkening waters, and the businessman – Jed, she reminded herself – turned his attention to the window, squinting against the sun's glare.

The colour still hadn't returned to his face, and when Amy lowered her gaze to his hands, she saw he gripped the leather seat rest between them, knuckles white.

She leaned her head back against the seat as he turned

away from the view, and closed her eyes for a moment, heart racing.

It wasn't meant to be like this.

Thank God it was a short flight.

Two hours, maybe less if they caught a tailwind.

Her attention snapped back at a low groan from the seat beside her, and she opened her eyes to see the man wiping his forehead with his fingers.

'Are you okay?'

He shook his head, then gave her a rueful smile. 'I'm a nervous flier.'

'Then why…?'

'It was a last minute change of plan. I usually drive up if I'm visiting over a weekend.'

'To Cairns?'

'Like I said, I hate flying.'

'Do you want some water?' Her finger hovered over the call button.

'No, no. That's all right. I don't want to make a fuss.' He swallowed, forced a smile. 'What's your name?'

'Amy Oliver.'

She bit her lip the moment the words passed her lips.

There was the first lie.

Stupid, she knew.

The more lies you told, the more chances there were of being caught, they'd told her.

She eyed the bag between her feet, the boarding pass tucked inside.

The one with a different name printed across it.

The man held out a hand as she straightened. 'Jed McIntyre.'

'Nice to meet you.' She returned the handshake, his grip weaker than she expected.

'Why are you flying to Cairns, Amy?'

'I'm visiting my parents. I couldn't get a flight at Christmas because I stupidly left it until the last minute, and then I couldn't get time off from work anyway.'

She held her breath, waited for the next inevitable question.

'What do you do?'

And there it was, right on cue.

'I'm a project administrator for an engineering company. Pipelines, things like that.'

Lie number two.

'It's not very exciting,' she added. 'What about you?'

'I'm a consultant. Self-employed.'

'Oh, doing what?'

His gaze hardened, then a split second later he smiled.

It didn't reach his eyes.

'I suppose you could say I introduce people who are interested in doing business together.'

Amy gestured to the business magazine in his lap, not wishing to push the matter. Not yet. 'An entrepreneur, then?'

The fuselage shook, and her stomach lurched as a woman cried out from the rear of the aircraft.

'Bloody hell,' Jed muttered, his grip tightening on the armrests.

'It always gets turbulent around here, especially after a storm,' said Amy while the pilot's voice filled the cabin, his soothing tone reminding everyone to wear their seat-belts. 'It's nothing to worry about.'

Jed shot her a sideways glance and swallowed. 'You're sure?'

'Absolutely. You should see what it's like on the Brisbane to Newcastle route. I spilt a gin and tonic in my lap on that flight once.'

He managed a chuckle, his hand moving to his shirt collar, loosening a button.

Amy reached into the seat pocket in front of her and retrieved the complimentary paper bag, smoothing its creases. 'Do you want this?'

'Not yet.' Jed gave her a sheepish smile. 'I'm not usually like this.'

'I'll bet. What are you doing when you get to Cairns?'

'Why?'

His smile was gone, a cold glare taking its place.

'Sorry, I didn't mean to be nosy.' She held up her hands to placate him. 'I was just trying to take your mind off the turbulence.'

'No, I'm sorry.' He took a deep breath, the fake smile back now. 'Just catching up with some friends, that's all.'

'Some time out?'

'That's it.' Jed grimaced as the turbulence decreased and a low ping accompanied the seatbelt lights going out. He unclipped his belt. 'Would you mind…?'

'Of course. I think the one this end is occupied though.' She pointed to the red light above their heads. 'Looks like you'll have to use one of the others.'

Scrambling from her seat, kicking her bag under the one in front so he didn't snag the strap on the way past and reveal its contents, she shuffled forward and watched while he made his way to the toilets at the back of the aircraft.

He grabbed at the back of seats as he walked, his gait unsteadied by the swaying motion of the aircraft while the turbulence dissipated.

Once he had disappeared into one of the cubicles, Amy dropped into her seat, legs shaking.

He hadn't recognised her, she was sure.

Chapter Three

Amy's fingers clawed at the strap of her backpack as she desperately trying to untangle it from the metal footrest folded up under the seat in front of her.

She gave it a final hard yank and sat back, gasping from the effort before peering over her shoulder.

There was no sign of Jed.

She opened it with a shaking hand, heart racing while she tried to locate her mobile phone amongst the borrowed purse, car keys, leather-bound diary with its empty pages…

Locating it underneath a tangled set of old earbuds and unravelling the wires that snagged around it, she angled the screen so she could read the last text message.

It gave her no comfort.

She was on her own, over five miles up in the air, and in a pressurised cabin.

She thumbed a brief update, then pressed send.

Putting the phone back in the bag, her fingertips brushed against cold steel, and sweat prickled at her brow.

Rachel Amphlett

Not yet, she reminded herself.

They said to do it once the aircraft had landed.

Not before.

Just in case.

Swallowing, throat dry, she watched as a teenager exited the toilet, waited until the girl had passed, then signalled to Sarah.

'Can I have some water please?' she asked, shoving the bag back under the seat.

The crew member nodded, her eyes widening before turning away.

'Jesus, the stench coming out of that place.'

Amy jumped at the sound of Jed's voice, then gave a wan smile as he towered over her.

'We've only been in the air forty minutes,' he continued, nodding his thanks as she moved out of his way. 'God knows what it'll be like by the time we land.'

'Here's your water.' Sarah returned, her gaze flitting to Jed. 'Anything for you, sir?'

'I'm fine.' He eyed the small plastic cup in Amy's hand and shook his head. 'I'd be careful how much of that you drink if I were you. I wasn't kidding about the toilet.'

Her choked laughter died on her lips at the sound of the curtain separating them from the economy seats followed by determined tiny footsteps, and then her heart lurched at the small voice beside her.

'Mummy!'

'God, I'm sorry – so sorry.' The child's father placed his hand on his daughter's shoulders, gently peeling her away from Amy's armrest. 'She's been visiting her mum in

144

Maroochydore this weekend… Angela looks just like you from the back… I'm sorry, she was looking for the toilet.'

Amy shook her head, forcing a smile. 'That's fine. It's okay, really.'

He breathed a sigh of embarrassed relief, then grinned at his daughter as he led her away. 'You can use the toilet at the other end, Lizzy. Come on, off we go.'

Turning away from the aisle, Amy drained the last of her water, scrunched up the cup and shoved it in the seat pocket hearing a satisfying crackle as the plastic yielded.

She bit back a sigh, aware that what came next, what surely had to follow would affect the lives of everyone on board the flight, including the little girl.

Should she stop?

Tell them it was a mistake, that she couldn't bring herself to carry out her mission?

What would be the ramifications when the man at the top found out?

A throaty grunt shook her from her jumbled thoughts.

'They're a handful at that age,' said Jed, shaking his head while he turned his attention back to his magazine, flicking over the page.

'Do you have kids?'

'Two, but they don't live with me.'

'Oh.'

'Trust me, their mother's welcome to them.' He glanced over. 'What about you?'

'Me?'

'Yes. Do you have kids?'

'No.' She rubbed at the skin where the wedding ring

used to be and forced a smile. 'Never say never though, right?'

Lie number three.

Chapter Four

The conversation died after that, and Amy spent the next forty-five minutes willing the aircraft to reach its destination as soon as possible.

Unknown to the crew, it would be the last flight they would take today.

She just wanted to get it over with now.

End it.

The turbulence returned to shake the cabin from side to side as they skirted past Townsville and Magnetic Island, the pilot's announcement at odds with the bright sunshine that flooded the left-hand side of the aircraft and bathed her ankles with welcome warmth.

Tearing her gaze away from Jed's fingers gripping the seat rest as he stared through the window, she closed her eyes while her thoughts turned to the past two weeks and a past filled with happiness, love and laughter.

Until the last day.

Today.

Why her?

Why now?

'Flight attendants, prepare for landing please.'

Amy grimaced and opened her eyes.

That damn pilot again.

Relaxed, confident, assured.

'I hate this part almost as much as taking off,' Jed muttered, peeling his hand from the leather and flicking through the final pages of his magazine, ignoring all the adverts squashed into the back pages and the flippant opinion column shoehorned onto the last page. 'Never again.'

'No more flights for you?' She couldn't resist a smile when Sarah and her colleagues leapt into action and began a well-practised march along the aisle, safety first and foremost in their minds while she carried *that* in her bag. 'What will you do instead?'

He shrugged. 'I don't know. Depends on the next couple of days, I suppose.'

'Well, whatever it is, I hope it goes well for you,' she lied.

Number four.

'What are you going to do when you get to Cairns?' Jed asked. 'You never said.'

'I haven't thought about it much,' came the easy reply.

Number five.

She cleared her throat. 'Well, actually I have. I thought I might spend the weekend in Port Douglas. I wasn't due back at work until Monday, so…'

'You'll love it there.' He shot her a dazzling grin.

'Do you know it well?'

'I've been there once or twice...' His good humour dissipated, a frown chasing away his smile. 'I'm heading up there myself actually.'

'Oh?'

He gave a slight shrug. 'A mate of mine's got a boat, that's all.'

'Nice. Is it big?'

'Forty-five feet.'

'Wow. Yes, I'd call that big. Where are you going?'

His top lip curled then, and he turned back to the window as the aircraft banked gently to the left, its engines changing tone as another alert beeped in the background while they started to lose altitude.

Amy bit back a curse, her ears popping. 'Sorry, I can't help being nosy sometimes. I...'

Stop.

Six lies would be pushing her luck.

And she needed as much of that as possible.

Especially now.

'Cabin crew, prepare for landing.'

'Thank Christ for that.' Jed flapped the magazine closed and tucked it into the elasticated pocket before tightening his seatbelt.

Amy's eyes fell upon the backpack beside his feet, and she chewed her lip.

Beyond the window, sunlight sparkled off the rolling waves chasing towards the Cairns beaches, and then they were banking again, lining up for the steep descent alongside the range of hills bordering the city.

Jed ran a hand across his jawline as they skimmed across car rental lots and eucalypt trees, and swore under his breath as the wheels smacked the tarmac.

Exhaling as the aircraft rapidly braked, Amy willed her heart rate to slow as she watched another aircraft taxiing into place for its departure.

Blood rushed in her ears, dulling Sarah's clipped instructions to passengers over the intercom, the flight attendant keeping a wary eye on the rest of the staff while she explained to passengers that there might be a delay in leaving the aircraft.

'Why?' Jed murmured.

Amy glanced out the window across the aisle to see the runway petering out, and then the aircraft swung left, accelerating forwards.

When she turned back to Jed, his gaze was fixed on a corrugated iron roofed hangar set away towards the perimeter of the airfield.

The doors were open wide, exposing a darkened maw where no light penetrated.

'Something's not right,' he said, twisting in his seat to peer through the reinforced glass. 'We're nowhere near the terminal.'

'What do you mean?' Amy tried to see past him, her skin crawling.

This isn't what they said would happen.

She gasped as three federal police vehicles emerged from the hangar at speed and drove straight towards the aircraft.

Gasps and murmurs filtered through the cabin as

passengers ignored Sarah's commands and rushed as one to peer through the windows.

Jed turned to face her, his green eyes filled with hatred.

'Shit,' they said in unison.

Then Amy unclipped her seatbelt and lurched for her bag, pulled out a Glock 9mm and aimed it at him.

Chapter Five

'Who the hell are you?' Jed snarled, eyeing the weapon hovering under his nose.

The couple in the row opposite cringed away, while a woman behind Amy's seat emitted a shocked scream.

'Amy Cornish.' She moved into the aisle and straightened her shoulders, emboldened by the weight of the gun in her hand. 'Australian Federal Police. Pass me the backpack. Slowly.'

As he bent over to retrieve it, Amy glanced over her shoulder. 'Sarah, I need you to pull the curtains.'

The crew member unbuckled her belt, the metal clasps clanging against her seat while her colleague's mouth formed a perfect "o".

She brushed past Amy, unhooking the curtains to shield them from the shocked faces of those in the economy section, then scrambled back to her seat, her bright red lipstick a stark contrast to her pale features.

The four remaining passengers in business class flinched when Amy glared at them.

'Stay in your seats. Don't move.'

When she turned back, Jed was holding the backpack against his chest, his gaze fixed on the exit door.

'Don't even think about it. I don't miss, so put the bag on the seat, and then put your hands on your head.'

A sudden jolt rocked the aircraft and she staggered sideways, the gun slipping from her grip.

Shock registered a split second before instinct took over, her body twisting while she fell, her gaze never leaving her target.

Jed pounced, sinews flexing as he lurched towards her, the backpack falling into her seat while his hands grasped at the empty space where she had been standing.

Her elbow clanged against the metal underside of the seat and she stifled a cry, desperately watching the gun's trajectory as it tumbled through the air, slid across the carpet and clattered to a standstill under the crew seats.

She rolled over, started to crawl towards it and then felt a strong hand wrap around her ankle.

Glancing over her shoulder, she saw an evil smile cross Jed's mouth.

'Got you,' he spat.

'Yeah, right.'

She flipped, lashing out with her foot at the same time, and heard the satisfying crunch of cartilage and soft tissue as her shoe found his nose.

He reeled backwards, bellowing.

Amy didn't hang around.

She scrambled towards the Glock, straightened and then planted her feet, her grip rock steady.

Breathing heavily, one hand on the back of a seat while

she cursed the sudden braking motion that had nearly ended her life, she watched as Jed tried to stem the flow of blood with his sleeve.

'You bitch,' he hissed.

Amy ignored him and instead tugged the backpack towards her, shaking it to loosen the zip.

It slid open, and she shuffled through the contents, her fingers caressing the bundles of cash lining the inside.

Then a light blue cotton shirt tumbled out, creased and bloodied.

A driving licence slipped from the breast pocket, an ugly stain obliterating the embossed signature but not the photograph or the details underneath.

She raised an eyebrow. 'What did you say your name was?'

'McIntyre.' His voice was muffled, thickened by blood and pain.

'That's interesting.' Amy flicked the licence around to face him. 'Because the body of a man matching McIntyre's description was found floating off a jetty on the Maroochydore river this morning, his ID missing along with half his face.'

The woman behind her emitted a frightened squeak before being shushed by her travelling companion.

Amy ignored them, too intent on watching the confidence slip from her quarry's face.

'Whereas you,' she continued, 'bear an uncanny resemblance to Taylor King, a drug dealer wanted in two States with an Interpol fan club demanding his extradition to France.'

King muttered under his breath, sagging further into his seat.

Amy smirked. 'Your mistake was leaving a trail from the boat ramp to the plane, including the gun you dumped in the smoking area outside the airport. What were you hoping to do, King – try to leave the country by boat once you got here?'

He mumbled something in response.

'I didn't catch that, King – speak up,' Amy said, ignoring the ruckus behind her as the exit door opened and three armed tactical officers stormed into the cabin.

'Vanuatu,' said King. He lowered his sleeve, glaring at her through red-rimmed eyes.

Amy frowned and reached into the backpack once more.

A chill shivered down her spine as her fingers touched hard plastic, and she pulled out a 3D printed gun.

King glowered at her. 'And I would have made it there without you.'

Chapter Six

Amy was bundled from the aircraft behind Taylor King, surrounded by armed men in bulky black bulletproof vests and carrying semi-automatic rifles.

In their wake, a cabin full of shocked passengers exploded with noise, demanding explanations and a hasty exit off the plane before her shoes touched the metal staircase and their voices faded away.

She reached the bottom of the stairs and watched while King was bundled into an armoured police vehicle and then whisked away, sirens blaring.

'Sergeant Cornish.'

She turned to see a burly man in his fifties approaching, and took a step backwards despite the pips on his shoulder epaulettes. 'Commander Granger.'

Confusion swept through her, and then she saw the familiar logo of a national television news channel emblazoned down the side of a van that was barrelling towards them.

'I hope they're not expecting to speak to me, sir.'

'Not at all. Come this way. Can I take that bag for you?'

'I'm fine, thanks.' Amy shifted the strap across her shoulder and glanced towards the plane. 'I need to be with my family. I need—'

'In a moment. Over here.' He steered her towards the shade of the hangar. 'Did King give any indication why he was flying up here after he killed McIntyre?'

'He said he was meeting some friends, and that one of them had a boat.'

'Right, okay. I'll have someone liaise with the city harbour patrol and send a couple of cars down to the marina. If he was meeting someone, we might still catch them before they realise he's not turning up.'

'Why didn't you arrest him before he boarded the flight, sir? Surely it would've been safer than this.'

'We didn't have a choice – King might've taken hostages given half the chance. If he did that, he could've got the pilot to take him anywhere he wanted and we wouldn't have been able to stop him. At least now we can interview him here and find out who his accomplices are. He might be willing to talk given that he was walking around with McIntyre's shirt.' Granger squinted against the bright sunlight streaming through the hangar door, and beckoned to one of his superintendents before turning back to Amy. 'We'll do a full debrief at district headquarters downtown at five o'clock but I'll let you get back to your family for now.'

'Thanks,' she managed. She handed him the Glock. 'And you can have this. I'm meant to be on holiday.'

Granger's eyes narrowed. 'You were the only one close enough at short notice.'

'That's what you said last time. You went too far today, sir. You put my family in danger.'

'We didn't.' He jerked his head towards the line of passengers disembarking from the aeroplane, their necks craning while they tried to catch a glimpse of what was taking place inside the hangar. 'They and everyone else on board that flight was safe, because of *you*. Thanks to you, we have one of Australia's biggest drug smugglers in custody.'

She glared up at him, met a steely gaze in response, and bit her lip.

'Sir, did you know that Taylor smuggled a 3D printed weapon through security?'

He paled beneath his brusque demeanour, then rubbed his chin. 'No. No, we didn't. Where is it now?'

'One of the armed response team took it into evidence with the shirt.' Amy crossed her arms while the commander squirmed.

'There'll be a full inquiry, of course.' Granger cleared his throat, pausing to inspect a large diving watch. 'But for now, you've got four hours until the debrief. We've arranged for a car to take you and your family to your hotel, and I'll send someone to collect you later. Don't be late.'

He turned, not waiting for her response, and evidently not expecting one.

Amy leaned against the hangar door, her legs shaking while the adrenalin ebbed away.

The aircraft was abandoned now, the crew standing

behind Commander Granger while he addressed a swelling group of journalists.

Passengers crowded towards the three buses approaching from the terminal, their heads bowed while they updated their social media, simultaneously marking themselves as "safe" while sharing their version of events, and eyeing the business class passengers with ill-disguised envy.

She shook her head in disgust, then spotted the man and the toddler walking towards her and smiled, relief feathering the first tentative acceptance of a job well done.

'Jesus, Morgan, am I glad to see you.'

'Mummy!'

'Oh my God, Carrie.' Amy swept the little girl into her arms as Morgan's arms wrapped around her shoulders.

The toddler pouted. 'Daddy called me Lizzy.'

'I'm sorry – she was off and running before I could stop her,' he murmured. 'I was so scared. When I saw him… All I could think of was for Chrissakes make up a name—'

'It's okay, don't worry. I'm safe, we're all safe.' She snuggled into his chest, clawing at his cotton shirt. 'It's done.'

'Until next time.' Morgan's face clouded.

'There won't be a next time. I'm quitting, as of now.'

He raised an eyebrow. 'Does Granger know?'

'Not yet.'

'Mummy, can we go snorkelling?'

Amy turned and buried her nose into her daughter's hair, the faint scent of mandarin shampoo enveloping her. 'We can do whatever you want to do, Carrie.'

Rachel Amphlett

Reaching out for Morgan, she wrapped her fingers around his and squeezed.

'Well done, love.' He grinned. 'And there was you telling me all these years that you're scared of flying.'

Amy managed a smile as she lowered Carrie to the ground.

'I wasn't lying about that,' she said, then swung Taylor King's backpack over her shoulder, tested the weight of the bundles of cash that shifted inside, and wondered how long it would take them to sail from Port Douglas to Vanuatu.

THE END

160

Special Delivery

Special Delivery

The van travelled through the silenced suburbs of the Somerset town.

Not too fast. Not too slow.

A solitary crisp packet tumbled across the road in front of the van, then stuck fast against the kerb and fluttered desperately against the wind that held it there.

Half past two in the morning.

November rain.

A faint mist clung to the urban sprawl, the unseasonal warmth giving up in the face of a drenching that increased in ferocity.

Dull orange sodium streetlights flashed off the roof of the panel van as it twisted and turned along a circuitous route.

It wasn't entirely alone.

A single decker bus, windows fogged up from the inside, trundled past in the opposite lane, the driver's face illuminated by the bright overhead lights, his expression grim with concentration.

Braking at the end of the road, the van turned left onto a street lined with terraced houses crammed next to each other, a mixture of exposed brick and painted plasterwork. Low stone walls provided a border between the homes and the pavement, a modicum of protection from the outside world.

The van continued onwards, past a Chinese takeaway with faded gold lettering above its door, past a laundrette that had long been abandoned, then under a railway bridge covered with graffiti tags that clung to the steel girders.

Wiper blades beat a steady rhythm across the rain-drenched windscreen, the rear lights from the vehicle in front reduced to red splats of colour by the next onslaught of water.

Jackson Dark reached out, twisted the plastic knob for the heating control, and notched it up a couple of degrees. The radio murmured in the background, some sort of late night political discussion that helped to silence the voices in his head.

He didn't listen to the programme.

Didn't care.

He flexed his fingers around the steering wheel, easing his foot off the accelerator a little as the van attempted to aquaplane through a deep puddle before correcting itself on the other side.

There was no rush now.

As long as the package was delivered before daybreak, that was all that mattered.

The mobile phone lit up in its cradle on the dashboard a split second before a familiar rock music track tore through the cab, evoking memories of a train journey to

London fifteen years ago and a lack of hearing for several days afterwards.

He pressed a button on the steering wheel.

'I'll be home in an hour or so.'

Margie sighed. 'The weather's atrocious out there. Be careful.'

'I will. Stop worrying. Go back to sleep.'

'I can't sleep.'

'You're not working at this hour, are you?'

'I thought I'd sit up and do the paperwork while you were out. Means we both get a day off tomorrow.'

The smile in her voice wrapped itself around him, and he turned down the radio.

'I thought we agreed you wouldn't. The invoicing will wait.'

'You can't do it all yourself, Jackson. It's all very well running your own business but I can help if you'd let me. You've got to learn to delegate.'

He chuckled.

She would never understand that there were some jobs that could never be delegated.

'I've got to go, love. I'm nearly there.'

He ended the call and tapped his fingers on the steering wheel as the rock music track continued in his head, the road undulating gently under the van, large semi-detached houses with manicured gardens now lining each side of the avenue as he passed.

A sudden flash of brown and white escaped from a garden and shot across the tarmac, the shape hunkered low to the ground.

Jackson clenched his teeth, and swerved across the

dotted white line in the middle of the street, thankful no traffic was coming the other way.

A scraping sound reached his ears from the back of the van and he swore under his breath as he braked.

The fox leapt between the steel bars of a garden gate on the opposite side of the road, its tail giving a warning flick as it disappeared from sight.

His heart racing, Jackson exhaled and steadied the vehicle as the street changed from residential to up-market commercial, wiping sweat from his forehead.

He checked his mirrors, and his heart missed a beat.

Blue flashing lights exploded from the dark behind, the police patrol car accelerating to catch up.

Jackson exhaled, indicated left and pulled to a stand-still at the kerb outside the darkened forecourt of a sports car dealership.

He had no interest in the gleaming silver specimen on display behind the reinforced glass though.

Reaching out for the button to lower the window, he blinked as horizontal rain struck him in the face and needled his eyes.

The police car had parked behind his, and now one of the occupants – he assumed there were two – climbed from the driver's side and jogged towards him. The officer's waterproof jacket did little to offset the fresh torrent that chose that exact moment to descend from the heavens.

Jackson managed to wipe the smirk off his face before the flashlight shone into his eyes, and raised his hand to ward off the glare.

'Evening, officer.'

'Were you aware your offside brake light isn't working?' said the police officer, lowering the beam so it fell to the dashboard.

'Isn't it?' Jackson rubbed his chin, fighting down the urge to panic. 'Sorry – must've blown a bulb when I braked for that fox. It was working fine this morning.'

The policeman's mouth thinned, and Jackson's heart sank.

'Mind if I take a look in the back of the van, sir?'

'What for?'

'Routine check. You've got a brake light out. Let's make sure there's nothing else wrong with the vehicle before we let you go. Last thing we want is to find you in a ditch later tonight, do we? Turn off the engine and get out of the vehicle, please sir.'

'Hang on.'

He turned away and reached out for the waxed jacket he'd discarded on the passenger seat, shrugged it over his shoulders and then pulled out a baseball cap he kept for emergencies from the glove compartment.

By the time he turned off the engine and climbed out, the police officer was wet through and glaring at him.

'The side door, sir?' he said through gritted teeth, and indicated with the torch beam that Jackson should lead the way.

'Sure.'

Sliding open the panel, Jackson took a cursory glance around the interior and then stood to one side to let the policeman pass.

The torch beam swept left and right, up the welded panels and across the fitted shelving Jackson had built near the driver's end of the vehicle.

On the floor, discarded boxes covered the surface, broken open and flattened and favouring the left-hand side where he'd swerved to avoid the fox.

'What is it you do, sir?'

'I'm a courier. Self-employed.'

'Where do you get most of your work from?'

'Online businesses. The usual suspects.' He jerked his chin at the empty packaging. 'All this will go to the Council recycling place tomorrow before I start my rounds. Costs a small fortune in fees.'

The torch beam swung over the flattened boxes, then stopped.

'Is there a storage compartment under here, sir?'

Jackson swallowed. 'Yes.'

'Care to open it up?'

He heaved himself into the back of the van, using his foot to clear away the packaging from the clips holding the floor panel in place.

Climbing out, he released the panel and slid it to one side.

The policeman stepped forward, his jaw tight as the torch beam illuminated the dark chasm under the floor.

'Flowers?'

'For my wife.' Jackson held up his hands. 'It's the only place I can hide the bouquet so she doesn't find them. It's our anniversary tomorrow. I want it to be a surprise.'

The policeman grunted, then switched off the torch. 'All right, close it up. Get back inside but don't start the engine.'

Jackson did as he was told, then sat with the window

down as the policeman took his details and began to write out the fixed penalty notice for the brake light.

Jackson glanced at his watch.

'Need to be somewhere, sir?' The policeman paused his note-taking and raised an eyebrow.

'No, it's just that the missus will be worried about me,' he said. 'It's been a long day.'

'Indeed it has, sir.' The policeman finished writing with a flourish of his pen, then tore off the carbon copy of the infringement notice and held it out. 'Make sure you get that fixed as soon as possible. It's not the weather for driving around in faulty vehicles.'

Jackson folded the notice and tucked it into his jacket pocket, then buttoned the flap to keep it safe. 'Okay if I go?'

'Certainly, sir. Drive safely now.'

Jackson wound up the window. Relieved that all the warmth hadn't been sapped from the vehicle, he flipped the switch to reheat the seats and blew on his hands to try to get the circulation working again.

In the door mirror, he saw the police car's indicator flash bright orange and then pull away from the kerb. He executed a mock salute at the occupants as they acceler-ated past.

The brake lights flared once at the end of the road, and then they were gone, lost to the rabbit warren of criss-crossing streets.

Jackson let his head fall back against the headrest for a moment, before reaching out and slipping the van into gear, his heart rate slowly returning to some semblance of normal.

After half a mile, he slowed to negotiate a roundabout offering three directions from which to choose, decided upon the third exit, then accelerated beyond the town's speed limit, ploughing onwards into the night.

The van slowed as the road began to climb upwards, the engine churning before finding momentum and surging ahead.

Jackson began to relax as the dark countryside wrapped itself around him, the van's headlights reflecting off butchered hedgerows that had been cut back at the end of October.

He flicked off the headlights, content to rely on the van's side lights and rested his foot on the brake pedal, gently easing the van to a slow crawl before turning right.

He didn't indicate.

The van purred past a large brick house on the corner of the junction, its front windows dark and its occupants oblivious to the night's activities.

Jackson fought down envy at the thought of warm blankets and central heating. He groaned as the wheels crashed into a deep pothole he mistook for a puddle, ruing the damage to the suspension that would eat into his profit, and hoping the noise would be shrouded by the pouring rain.

Naked horse chestnut trees and ancient oak nestled on either side of the lane, which deteriorated with every twist and turn.

He braked the van to a slow crawl as he approached two ramshackle corrugated iron machinery sheds on the opposite side of the lane to a house behind a low fence.

The lane widened before straightening out, and he

checked the clock on the dashboard as the van passed a T-junction, a white signpost flashing by the passenger window.

Plenty of time yet and no need to hurry, despite what he had told the policeman.

He jumped at movement out the corner of his eye at the side of the road, then swore as he realised the faces belonged to sheep who peered out from behind the wire fence that kept them corralled in the field.

It always happened like this.

The closer he got, the more nervous he became.

After another minute, the lane dropped below a railway bridge, the Victorian brick structure providing a split second's respite from the rain before spitting him out the other side.

He could see it then, or at least sense it.

The side lights no longer picked out a hedgerow but instead a black expanse that disappeared into the night.

The reservoir clung to the landscape, its depths ice cold, remorseless.

Jackson swallowed as the headlights picking out the flash of a red post box next to the turning for the Norman church, uncomfortable at the close proximity of something so holy to something so—

He pushed the thought aside.

Nearly there.

Half a mile, and he turned the van to the left, bouncing it through soft gravel that sucked at the tyres and hampered his progress.

When the sidelights picked out the dark water's edge, he stopped and applied the handbrake.

His fingers found the zip of his waxed jacket and he pulled it up to his chin, tugging the baseball cap firmly onto his head before releasing the door handle.

The wind buffeted him against the side of the van, and he threw out his arms to regain his balance, shocked by the assault. He steadied himself and made his way around to the side of the vehicle, then reached out and released the side door once more.

Climbing in, he began to gather up the flattened boxes and stack them against the far side, clearing the floor of the van. Once finished, he lowered himself back to the ground.

He ignored the compartment he'd opened for the policeman and instead peeled back the black rubber water-proof lining.

Jackson let out an exasperated sigh.

The sudden swerve he'd executed to avoid the fox had sent the package flying across the floor of the van, exactly as he'd suspected.

At the far end of the recess between the wheel arches, he could just make out the black plastic wrapped around the lifeless form, the bin liners secured in place with duct tape.

He groaned as he eased himself up into the van, ruing the backache that plagued him on a regular basis, slipped his hand into the cavity, and reached out for the body.

The client had assured him that the package wasn't big, and he wasn't wrong.

The problem was the bricks that had been included. They added several kilogrammes, which shifted with every movement.

Sweating under the thick coat, Jackson dragged the

package from the recess until he'd managed to get the bulk of it exposed, then climbed out and slung the body over his shoulders in a fireman's grip before staggering towards the reservoir's shoreline, grunting as he waded in.

Ice cold water slapped at his rubber boots and he squinted in the faint beam from the van's sidelights, keen to avoid going too deep. He knew these waters well – a steep shelf cleaved away from a gentle slope only a metre or so from where he stood.

Once he was sure he had the right position, he heaved the body into the water and took a step back, panting.

The package began to sink straight away, the bricks carrying it beneath the depths, the water obliterating any trace of the person inside.

He didn't know who it was.

Didn't care.

Bubbles popped to the surface, a final gurgle escaping from the parcel before it sank completely.

Jackson turned away and made his way back to the van.

He needed to get those flowers in some water before they started to dehydrate.

She'd be delighted he remembered.

As he slid the side panel closed, his hand brushed the liveried paintwork that covered the side of the vehicle, the black stencilling underneath the courier logo stark against the white paint.

Special deliveries our speciality.

THE END

A Pain in the Neck

A Pain in the Neck

A cool pale light threads its fingers between the metal slats of the white venetian blinds, feeling its way over the painted window sill.

The sunbeam stops when it reaches the bed, becoming shackled by an expensive wristwatch of diamonds and gold that glistens as its owner folds his arms under his head and lets out an anguished groan.

'Relax, Charlie. If you fight me, you know you're only going to make it hurt all the more.'

I flex my fingers and rest my thumbs either side of Charlie Petersen's spine and press gently at the base of his thick neck, just under the grey curling hair that he tends to wear on the long side, even in his advancing years.

'Here?'

'Yes, oh yes.'

A smile twitches at the corner of my mouth.

Charlie Petersen is a sixteen stone giant of a man but when pain seizes his back with the wrath of a demon, he's like putty.

My thumbs sink into the pasty soft skin of his shoulders and he lets out an agonised cry that drowns out the panpipes and rainfall emanating from the speakers on top of a beech-coloured cabinet behind the door to the treatment room.

I chuckle, slide my hands across his skin, and repeat the motion, sweeping my fingers between his shoulder blades and squeezing each of his vertebrae in turn.

Charlie turns his head, burying his face into the paper towel lining the hole at the top of the bed, and chokes back a scream.

I hum under my breath as I work my way down until I reach the dip of his pelvic bone, and then start work on his right hip.

His body writhes as he tries to shuffle away from the pain, but I don't stop. Instead, I grit my teeth and point my elbow deeper into the dense muscles, pushing my heels into the carpet to lend more weight to the manoeuvre.

Charlie lets out a whimper before I switch to the other hip, brushing my fingertips over the tattoo that runs from his rib cage to his thigh, and then he groans through gritted teeth as my thumbs find the nerves under the skin.

I let him rest, stepping back from the table and cracking my knuckles before wiping some of the oil from my hands with a soft clean white towel while I assess the prone figure.

Eventually, Charlie raises his head from the table and twists his neck until he faces me, cheeks burning beneath pale blue eyes, a red indent circling his face from where he's been lying against the padded headrest.

At five foot nine inches tall and after years of cheap alcohol and junk food, he's all fat and atrophied muscle.

I can count at least three chins folding down to his stump of a neck, and resist the urge to curl my lip in disgust at the thin line of drool that hangs from his mouth.

He blinks, then wipes it away with the back of his hand. 'That hurt.'

'I'm not surprised. When was the last time you came to see me? Six months ago?'

'You know how busy Trevor keeps me.' He tries to look contrite, and fails. 'Very busy.'

'You need to come and see me at least every six weeks to keep on top of this.'

'I can't, Vanessa. You don't understand.'

I drop the towel on the chair beside the square table that serves as my desk and scan the coloured squares across the screen of my tablet computer. 'April. April the fifteenth. That's when you were last here. That's why it hurts.'

'I'm too busy.'

His voice adopts a familiar whining tone, the one he uses when I tell him my prices have gone up or, like now, that he needs to take better care of his ageing body.

'Nobody is too busy, Charlie.'

He attempts to sit up, thinks better of it and slumps back to the headrest, his arms dangling either side of the bed. 'Try telling that to Trevor.'

Not likely.

The panpipes and rainfall ends, and now we're in a meadow with a bee buzzing around and cows lowing in the background.

It's a strange choice for a relaxation playlist but I refuse to pay for the premium version of the app, so I put up with the advertisements as well.

'Look, maybe you should try Pilates. It's good for strengthening your core muscles. It'll help support your back. What do you think?'

'I don't know if I should. That's for girls, isn't it?'

'No, it's for everyone. Have a think about it, at least. I can recommend someone who teaches classes locally. She's discreet.'

'Okay, maybe.'

'Have you been remembering to lift properly, like I showed you last time? Bending your knees, not using your back?'

'The problem is, they struggle. You only need one of them to shift their weight when you're trying to carry them or hold their head underwater and that's it – my back goes into spasms.'

I advance towards the bed and his eyebrows shoot upwards.

'I haven't finished yet, Charlie.'

'But—'

Whatever he was going to say is cut off by the yelp that escapes his lips as I dig my thumbs into his right hip again.

I can feel the knot in the muscle taunting me, trying to move under the skin, away from my touch.

'You're too tense. Try to relax.'

A muffled response reaches my ears and I glance up.

He's got his face buried in the paper towel again. As if

realising I couldn't understand, he turns his head to one side and tries again.

'I can't relax. It went wrong last time.'

My fingers hover above the tattoo. 'What?'

'I told you. My back gave out. The bastard managed to get away.'

'What did Trevor say?'

'I don't think he knows. I haven't told him yet.'

'Oh, Charlie.'

I go to work on his shoulders, pummelling the folds of skin to warm the muscles before I start work on his neck, easing my thumbs up and down his spine.

He's unaware that I'm moving towards the head of the bed, changing my position so that my hands are now caressing his skull.

I encircle his head with my arm, my elbow under his chin.

He stiffens.

'Trust me, Charlie.'

I brace my wrists, and twist.

There is a satisfying crunch as muscles loosen, and he sags within my grasp.

'You're right, I should come here more often.'

'We'll make an appointment for you as soon as I'm finished.'

I can feel his body starting to relax now, and his breathing slows as I work away from the pain points of his hips and spine and concentrate on massaging out the last of the kinks from his ageing frame before I return to his neck.

By the time he realises something is wrong, I've already got him in a vice-like grip.

181

He gurgles once and then I twist once, hard.

I hear it, the snap of muscle and bone as his neck breaks instantly.

I'm wiping my hands on the soft white towel when the door opens and Trevor Benedict peers in, eyebrow cocked.

'Did he struggle?'

'No.' I smile.

'Good. That's one less pain in the neck I have to worry about.'

THE END

The Last Days of Tony MacBride

The Last Days of Tony MacBride

As I hear the opening bars of music spew from the organ, I know I'm in trouble.

The key is one I can't sing – I've either got to squawk like a crow or do my best Johnny Cash impression, and neither is going to go down well with the woman in the front pew, her hand shaking as she holds the service programme for her husband's funeral.

She knows every word, of course. We're both regular churchgoers, but her visits are from a sense of religious fervour and guilt.

My visits come with the job.

My name is Allan O'Reilly, owner of O'Reilly and Sons.

Funeral director.

It's an unimaginative business name, but I inherited it from my dad so it's not like I had any choice in the matter.

I clear my throat and join in with the chorus, my voice little more than a murmur. At least my lips are moving in time with everyone else, even if the minister gives me a sideways look that tells me he's not convinced.

The caterwauling reaches an uneven crescendo. The congregation battles with the organist, who is intent on wrenching every last note from his instrument of torture until he finishes, and we fall back into our seats, exhausted with the effort.

As they sit, I reach into my collar and scratch at the label in my shirt that has been tickling my neck for the past ten minutes. It's newly purchased, especially for this occasion.

I try to make an effort for my clients.

I hear my name, and the minister gestures to me. It's my turn.

I fix a benevolent smile on my lips and begin to read the eulogy for Miriam MacBride's husband.

I wrote it myself.

It took me three late nights and half a bottle of dark rum, but I got there in the end.

I glance up.

Miriam is staring at me.

My voice falters and I clear my throat while the minister rests his hand on my arm and tells me to take my time.

I try not to snort out a manic laugh at the absurdity of it all, the effort causing my eyes to water, and then that sets everyone else off. The people in the front row are dabbing their cheeks with paper tissues, a few muffled sobs reaching my ears.

You see, I knew Tony MacBride.

Better than most.

A large man, his suits could have burst from his frame if not for the handmade quality of the material and a generous cut to the cloth.

Tony knew how to invest, how to spot an opportunity – and how to hold a grudge.

He began his working life selling used sports cars. The garage wasn't far from here, in a nondescript town that carried the stench from the local abattoir across its rooftops most days in August. A hardworking man, he had the gift of the gab and a network of acquaintances who could get things done.

Tony soon gained a reputation as a man who could fix things.

The garage expanded over time to include a service workshop, tucked around the back of the low-slung property so as not to detract from the gleaming vehicles in the showroom that faced the road.

Me and my mates used to peer through those showroom windows on our way home from school, shielding our eyes as we drooled over the cars we could never afford and would never drive.

Three days after my sixteenth birthday, I got a part-time job at the garage. I was scrawny then, a mere scrap of a lad but Tony saw something in me and gave me a chance.

I swept floors, sorted the stock of spare parts, and soon found myself apprenticed to an elderly mechanic with a shock of nicotine-tainted white hair.

I loved the scent of grease and motor oil, the clamour of eighties pop songs blaring on the radio competing with the clang and clatter of tools upon metalwork. On Fridays,

I'd help in the spray booth wearing a mask against the paint fumes, watching and learning as the experts worked.

Within two years, I'd qualified and taken over additional duties.

Tony would wander out from his office to the service bays for the important jobs, the ones involving less prestigious vehicles but requiring as much care and attention to detail.

These were the cars that arrived in the small hours, under cover of darkness and a tarpaulin.

He would place his suit jacket on a hanger that could always be found on a hook behind his office door, then roll up the sleeves of his shirt and stand, arms folded over his chest while we toiled through the night.

He trusted the men who worked for him, trusted their workmanship at turning something like a blue four-door family saloon into a red version of a model two years older, all within twenty-four hours.

Then, another acquaintance of his would arrive to take the vehicle away, a man who stayed in the shadows and kept his face from prying eyes. He would return two days later with a fat envelope, the contents of which would be divided among us once Tony took his share.

In the summer months, Tony would close the garage early on a Friday afternoon, tie an apron around his waist and hand out cold bottles of beer while a barbecue hissed and spat sausage fat outside the doors of the service area.

We'd play cricket then, the sound of the willow bat against a leather ball echoing off the walls, Tony umpiring with gusto.

At Christmas, his bonuses were generous. He'd take us

to one side to check everything was okay at home, at work, in life.

You see, Tony valued loyalty above everything else.

Insisted on it.

Demanded it.

He knew my dad, too.

They'd been friends at school since the age of six and Dad would often peer into the service bays to greet me before disappearing into Tony's plush office, shutting the door behind him. Every now and again, raucous laughter would filter through, and then Dad would emerge once more, Tony slapping him on the back in farewell.

Tony spent a lot of time behind that closed door, making his deals, planning his next investment.

Miriam would sweep in every now and again – a blast of expensive perfume followed by a jangle of gold jewellery and a swish of silk. She wouldn't stay long, just enough to make her presence known, get her bank account topped up with another cheque from Tony, and then off she'd totter in her six-inch high heels to the shiny new cabriolet parked at the kerb.

In my younger days, I'd fantasise about her – until Tony took me to one side and left me with no illusions what would happen if I tried anything.

He loved her it seemed, despite her faults.

Everything changed when my Dad died, and I took over the running of his business.

I kept in touch with Tony over the years, our paths crossing from time to time as the need arose – nothing more, nothing less.

The garage continued to offer repairs and sales by day

and kept a busy trade in alternative services by night. Local councillors extolled Tony's exuberance for employing the town's youth, especially those who might have otherwise shunned work for other nefarious activities.

And Miriam continued to flirt with the new apprentices.

I inhale the scent of fresh flowers filling the front of the church.

Lilies, of course and then the carnations – always a favourite of Tony's and a permanent fixture in his jacket buttonhole no matter the season or day of the week. Someone has ordered lilacs, a dark contrast to the white roses woven into the wreath with ivy tresses.

Arranged around the threadbare russet-coloured carpet below the flower display are white envelopes – cards of condolence that weren't posted to the house, and donations to Tony's favourite charity for greyhound rescue.

I blink and raise my gaze from the piece of paper in my hand.

At least forty pale faces peer at me, some craning their necks to get a better view.

As the curtains sweep closed, shielding the coffin from view and the first notes of Puccini's *Nessun Dorma* are broadcast over our heads, Miriam MacBride weeps loudly, lamenting her loss. She turns to the woman next to her – her sister – and proclaims her undying love for Tony.

It's a shame Tony's not around to see it all.

He'd be tickled pink.

You see, Tony MacBride is now Martin Broadshaw, and currently en route to Malaga.

His wife is oblivious to the fact that the man she's been

having an affair with for the past year is now being whisked towards the furnace instead, dead these seven days past, the victim of a blow to the back of the head with a cricket bat.

I can still feel the weight of the willow bat, still hear the wet thud as it met his brain.

Like I said, Tony MacBride demands loyalty.

He knows how to hold a grudge.

And he has a network of acquaintances who can get things done.

THE END

The Moment Before

The Moment Before

Ray Holden cranked open the tinted glass door, then stepped onto the balcony and took a deep breath.

He always loved the view from up here.

At night, he could see the sparkle and flare from the neon signs peppered across the tops of buildings in Canary Wharf while he listened to the laughter and soft clink of glasses from the tables outside the tapas restaurant down the road.

A full moon on the rise would straddle the skyscrapers, bathe the city in a cool light that eased away from the shadows and halted conversations as people paused to stop and stare, raise their phones and try to capture the moment.

This afternoon was different though.

A lethargy seeped into the city suburb, curling its way around the apartment blocks.

Traffic was quiet, save for the occasional delivery truck or cyclist zipping past.

The balconies to either side of him were devoid of life, the neighbours at work or running errands.

The one on his left – owned by a single woman who worked as a paralegal if his information served him right – held a wrought-iron table and chairs while the glass safety panels were obscured by a variety of herbs growing in colourful pots.

He inhaled the aromas. Basil, oregano, garlic – there was rosemary in there somewhere, too.

He wondered if she cooked, what her signature dish might be.

Something Italian perhaps.

Turning to the balcony on his right, he noticed a discarded off-white teddy bear with one eye missing as it stared up at the blue sky with the other. The glass barrier was covered in stickers, and he wondered which poor sod would have the job of trying to remove those when the family outgrew its home.

Ray's gaze travelled to the park opposite the apartment block at a child's cry.

Two toddlers screeched with delight as they were pushed on swings by their mothers while a commercial airliner banked high in the sky above them as it took off from the city airport.

In the distance, a dog howled as a police siren passed before falling silent.

He wrapped his fingers around the steel guard rail, his knuckles white.

Everything seemed so normal.

And yet—

His doctor told him last week that he needed to relax, quickly followed by a warning that if he didn't, then Ray wouldn't see Christmas because he was so stressed.

His heart couldn't take it.

Ray left the doctor's office and resolved to deal with the stress in his life.

Immediately.

Starting with Joe McAvoy.

Seven years ago, Joe was a zit-covered eighteen-year-old desperate to impress.

After starting as a bartender at one of Ray's nightclubs, he'd quickly risen to the role of supervisor, his smooth delivery of just the right amount of bravado and cheekiness endearing him to Ray.

He'd become like a son, especially to Marcie who was still mourning the fact she couldn't have children twenty years after the news.

Within three years, Ray handed over some of the smaller deals to Joe and watched while the younger man's confidence grew alongside a fearsome reputation that, along with Ray's blessing, forged a partnership that took the business from strength to strength.

But kids didn't always turn out the way you wanted them to, did they?

Ray turned to face the sumptuous living room and loosened his tie as he leaned against the guard rail, the late autumn sun warming the back of his neck.

Inside, the walls were covered with framed posters – old jazz gigs from way back, long before the current tenant had been born. A large black and white photograph of the New York skyline took up the entire space above the television, and he wondered if it was placed there as a goal – or a pipe-dream.

A thick mink-coloured carpet covered the floor, one that Ray knew cost upwards of five thousand pounds.

Cash, of course.

Because that's how Joe did business.

Safer that way.

Or so he thought.

Running his gaze over the open-plan kitchen and diner, squinting as the gleaming appliances caught the sun, Ray wondered when it started to go wrong.

His ears were still ringing from all the shouting moments earlier. He hated confrontation but it seemed to seek him out on purpose, testing his patience.

Testing his nerves.

Testing his resolve not to reach into his jacket pocket and light up a cig—

No, he wouldn't.

He quit.

A whole week ago, in fact.

When he left the doctor's office.

And without the aid of those little sticky patches that tore the hairs off your arms.

Trying to give up the little white sticks was killing him but Marcie kept nagging and no matter what he did, she could pick up the smell of nicotine on him at fifty paces.

If he were honest, Marcie's rage was a more frightening prospect than cancer.

Ray concentrated on the breathing techniques his doctor had shown him last week and turned back to the street below.

Inhale through the nose over a count of four.

Exhale through the mouth over a count of eight.

There.

Better.

The kids were in their pushchairs now, the mothers nattering away as they walked towards the exit opposite the apartment block, not a care in the world, their laughter drifting up to where he surveyed his kingdom.

A helicopter buzzed across the farthest reaches of the park, its red livery identifying it as a radio station's aircraft as it turned away. High enough not to break any laws, low enough to report on traffic flow in between the advert breaks and chit-chat.

His mobile phone pinged.

Pulling it from his jacket pocket, his eyes skimmed the text.

He says he gave the goods to Mack. Says he got a better price.

Ray's jaw clenched as he eyed the plastic bags on the sofa, the ones containing eighty thousand pounds, all in tens and twenties.

Used.

Money that should have been his.

Joe always had enjoyed the perks of the job.

A little too much.

The expensive suits, the wining and dining, the flash cars.

Despite all that, Joe said he put the money aside, saved it for a rainy day and that the merchandise was still in the warehouse awaiting collection.

The moment before Nick and Neil had taken Joe McAvoy kicking and shouting from the apartment and up the fire escape stairs, Ray almost believed him.

The moment before the text message, he was starting to have doubts.

The moment before, he thought he could trust his business partner.

Ray's thumb hovered over the screen a moment longer, then typed two words.

Do it.

He hit the send button, tucked the phone back in his pocket and sighed.

Seven years.

Seven years they'd been running their drugs operation without a hitch.

Seven years before Joe McAvoy double-crossed him for the first and last time.

Ray inhaled the neighbour's herbs, his fingers twitching towards the crumpled packet in his jacket pocket, the one holding the single cigarette he kept for emergencies.

He heard a shout, the sound of a struggle several floors above McAvoy's apartment.

Pigeons squawked, the beat of panicked wings reminding him of belated applause that echoed off the façade.

A split second later a man's body tumbled past him, right between the two balconies, his expensive suit jacket flapping in the wind.

Speed, mass, a muffled *clang* as McAvoy's forearm caught against the guard rail of the balcony below, then—

Ray didn't watch the body hit the pavement, but he heard it.

Heard the grapefruit-like crush of bones and sinew and skin and muscle as it met concrete.

Heard the screaming begin after the two women with pushchairs turned to see what the noise was.

He closed the floor-to-ceiling glass doors and crossed the plush carpet.

Picked up the plastic bags, testing the weight in his grip, rolling his shoulders to counter the slight tremble in his arm muscles.

Locked the front door, handed the keys to Nick – or was it Neil? Always hard to tell with identical twins.

Followed the twins to the emergency exit stairs. Removed the protective gloves that masked his fingerprints.

Reached the underground car park and climbed in the back of the sleek four-by-four with the smoked glass passenger windows.

Smiled as he removed the last cigarette from the packet and crushed it between his fingers.

The moment before, he was tempted to light it.

The moment before, he remembered his doctor's words.

The moment before, the stress in his life had passed him by.

THE END

THE END

Nowhere to Run

A Detective Kay Hunter short story

Chapter One

'You're not going to puke, are you?'

Probationary Detective Constable Kay Hunter
clenched her takeaway coffee cup between her fingers and
looked at the pitiful sight that lay spreadeagled on the bike
path.

A biting early April chill cut across the council-
managed park, trees see-sawing back and forth as she
peered at the outer cordon of blue-and-white crime scene
tape and narrowed her eyes at a cluster of onlookers
craning their necks, hungry for details.

A dozen uniformed police officers with grim expressions patrolled the perimeter and demanded formal statements from those who hovered at the fringes despite the
early hour.

Kay gritted her teeth and resisted the overwhelming
urge to kick the senior detective crouching next to the
body at her feet.

Ex-military police, Detective Sergeant Devon Sharp's
reputation and no-nonsense approach to his casework

sometimes jarred with the younger officers assigned to him, and Kay had no wish to start her investigative career with Kent Police on the wrong foot.

'No, Sarge,' she managed. 'I'm not. I've seen plenty of dead bodies before. Doesn't mean it doesn't affect me though.'

Weak sunlight broke through the boughs of the beech trees lining the concrete path and cast a tattoo of shadows over the victim's bare legs, one running shoe lying sideways underneath a nearby wooden bench.

The flies were already gathering, their incessant buzzing a white noise beneath the murmured voices of Kay's colleagues.

She concentrated on inhaling the rich aromatic fumes of caffeine laced with two sugars and glared at the older constable who stood opposite her, an ill-disguised smirk across his lips. He coughed and looked away, but not before she saw a grin crease his mouth.

Kay swore under her breath and imagined how satisfying it'd be to dump her coffee over the smug—

'Hunter, take a look at this.'

Her gaze returned to the dead female jogger.

The Acting Senior Investigating Officer, Detective Sergeant Devon Sharp, lifted the dead woman's arm, turning it gently between his gloved hands.

Kay placed her coffee cup on the concrete path and then donned gloves and protective overalls before lifting the crime scene tape and squatting next to him.

The victim was dressed in calf-length running tights and a singlet vest top.

Kay had found a baseball cap under a nearby shrub and carefully placed it in a plastic evidence bag.

The baseball cap had likely tumbled from the victim's head the moment her skull had caved in with the force of the blow that had ultimately killed her, according to the forensic pathologist who now hovered beside Sharp, head bowed.

Kay reckoned he was right.

That was how the last victim had been killed.

Sharp pointed to the empty cotton smartphone holder strapped to the woman's upper left arm.

'Just like the last one, Sarge,' she said.

'Indeed.'

He stood and began barking orders to the team, sending the junior constable and his colleagues to walk a perimeter to see if they could find the missing phone.

Kay knew it would be a fruitless task.

The killer had been too clever for that.

The pathologist, Lucas Anderson, nodded to her as he passed, snapping latex gloves from his fingers. 'I'll be in touch once I have a day and time confirmed for the post mortem, Hunter.'

'Thanks.'

As Kay dealt with the questions fired at her by the team and made sure she followed procedure at the crime scene, she noticed a blue van being driven across the park towards them.

It slowed as it neared, and then the engine died and the doors opened.

Two figures in white paper suits climbed from the vehicle, hurried to the back doors, and extracted four metal cases before slamming the doors and making their way up the small incline to where she stood next to the victim.

The crime scene investigators.

Specifically, Hugh Hughes and Amber Holstein.

Hugh managed to look like a geek no matter what he wore, due to his shaggy, brown fringe hanging over his glasses. His height meant that he always appeared to be looking down his nose at people, a trait that had the unfortunate tendency to be confirmed once he opened his mouth.

Amber's long blonde hair was tied back and bagged under a paper hat, but the trainee pathologist still managed to wear her work clothes as if she was walking down a catwalk.

Kay peered down at her own crumpled protective clothing and bit back a sigh.

'Morning!' Hugh chirped as they reached the bike path.

Amber set her case down on the floor next to the victim, rubbed her gloved palms together, then turned her back to Kay. 'The killer's left another one for us then, Devon?'

Kay exhaled slowly as the DS brought the pair up to speed.

'Right, right,' the pathologist nodded. 'Well, okay then. Let's take a look at her.'

Kay turned her back and walked a few discreet paces away while the team worked and contemplated the investigation to date – one that had now been made more complicated by the discovery of a second victim.

The first murder had been discovered seven days previously, in a park only four miles away.

The second murder was only six days before the town's charity run. Constant pressure would come from both Headquarters and the local district council as she and her colleagues tried to assure the public that the town remained safe, while the media would go wild with speculation.

Kay glanced over her shoulder to see Amber working beside the dead woman, and scowled.

She needed more coffee.

Chapter Two

Kay bit back a yawn and glared at the whiteboard.

A sickly sheen covered its surface, the poor lighting in the incident room lending a green tinge to the black markings on the board.

The clack of fingertips on keyboards, shouted requests for urgent reports and muted telephone conversations created a cacophony within the low-ceilinged space, and she wrinkled her nose at the hours-old stench of instant noodles and energy drinks that lingered in the air.

Her gaze flickered over the map that Sharp had pinned to a corkboard, the two victims' places of work and their homes circled with a red felt-tip pen.

Various points of interest had been identified across the map, including where the two victims had been known to shop regularly, attend a gym, and socialise with friends.

'Let's get on with this, and then you can get yourselves home.'

She turned at the sound of Sharp's familiar ex-military bark, then scurried to find a seat near the front of the gathering officers and turned to a new page in her notebook as he began the briefing.

'We have a positive identification for our victim from this morning. Laura Scott, thirty-two – worked as a dental hygienist at a practice in Bearsted. Her pink top was recognised by another runner who went past the crime scene at a distance and who then spoke to one of the officers on duty at the cordon. Apparently, Tanya Green attends the same gym Laura went to and says that they used to meet for coffee after a Sunday morning Pilates class.' Sharp waited while the assembled officers caught up with their note-taking. 'Understandably, Miss Green was shaken up by Laura's murder but has given us some useful information to get us started.'

'Did she know our other victim, Sarah Anderson, Sarge?'

The words were past Kay's lips before she could stop them, and she felt heat rise to her cheeks as all her colleagues turned to her. 'Sorry, Sarge.'

'Not a problem – I'd rather hear your questions as we go along rather than have you forget something at the end.' Sharp gave a faint smile. 'But I'd prefer it if you gave me a chance to get going first.'

Laughter rippled through the incident room, and Kay lowered her gaze to her notebook.

'In answer to Kay's question, no – Miss Green couldn't confirm if Laura knew Sarah, and hadn't heard of Sarah's name beyond last week's news reports.' Sharp glanced down at his notes before continuing. 'Who's currently going through Sarah Anderson's social media accounts?'

'Me, Sarge.' A detective constable by the name of

Bradley Thomas raised his hand. 'Do you want me to take a look at Laura's accounts as well?'

'Please – and let me know if you find anything that suggests they knew each other. Kay, I want you to head over to the gym that Tanya Green mentioned and speak to the manager there. In particular, find out whether Sarah was a member as well. In any event, I want to know if he's received any complaints of harassment from his female clientele from other members of the gym.'

'Will do, Sarge,' said Kay, scribbling a note.

'Uniform have spent the morning interviewing Laura's neighbours and immediate family,' Sharp continued. 'I want a review of those statements, as well as those of her friends and work colleagues – see if there is anything that gives you cause for concern, or whether there's anyone who links her to Sarah Anderson. We'll reconvene tomorrow after the post mortem results are received. Dismissed.'

As the team dispersed back to their desks, PC Simon Higgins wandered over to Kay and handed her another sheaf of paperwork still warm from the photocopier.

'That's the last of the witness statements to add to the ones you've already got,' he said. He glanced over his shoulder to where Sharp was speaking with two more experienced detectives, then turned back to her and lowered his voice. 'Do you think it's a serial killer?'

Kay wrinkled her nose. 'It's a bit too soon to say that.'

'Two women, both joggers, both bashed over the head with a blunt instrument? Got to be connected, haven't they?'

She shrugged, unwilling to concede that the same

thought had occurred to her during the briefing. 'Best get the evidence to suggest that before we start assuming anything, Simon. Always safer that way, in case we over-look anything, right?'

'I suppose so. Do you want me to come with you to do that interview at the gym in the morning?'

'That'd be good, thanks.' She smiled, recognising the same eagerness to be involved in an active investigation that she had felt before passing her detective's exams earlier that year. 'Meet in the car park at eight?'

'Okay, great.'

Higgins walked away with a bounce in his step.

Kay turned her attention to the pile of witness statements on the desk beside her, a sad collection of stories and memories of happier times.

'Have you eaten anything today?'

Kay jumped in her seat at the sound of Sharp's voice, knocking the witness statements to the floor, then turned to face him, her face aflame.

'I-I, no. No, I haven't, Sarge.'

Kay bent down and began pulling the paperwork across the worn carpet, gathered it all together, and placed the documents back on the desk.

When she looked up, Sharp was smiling, not unkindly.

'It's been a long day,' he said. 'And we're going to be busy tomorrow. Go home.'

'Thanks, Sarge.'

Chapter Three

Kay unlocked the communal door to the block of flats and stepped into a narrow hallway, the aroma of freshly cooked food wafting under the door to the ground-floor flat.

As she climbed the staircase, a television played in her neighbour's home on the next floor, the sound of a car chase and automatic weapons following her along the landing.

After she turned her key in the new lock she'd had fitted the day after moving in a year ago, she flicked on lights as she moved through her flat, threw her bag onto a threadbare sofa that was too comfortable to replace, and kicked off her shoes under an occasional table in front of it. Stretching her arms above her head and letting out an enormous yawn, Kay wandered into the bedroom and eyed the running shoes beside the wardrobe door.

The walls shook with another movie explosion.

It was all the motivation she needed.

Throwing her suit trousers and shirt into the washing basket next to the door, she pulled on her running kit before heading back into the living room, placed her phone into the armband around her left bicep and tucked her keys into her sweatshirt pocket.

In two minutes, she was outside and easing into her training route around Tonbridge's northern suburbs, some of the frustration from the investigation disappearing as she broke into long strides.

Following Higham Lane, she headed towards the Hadlow Road and the sound of diminishing commuter traffic. She fell into an easy pace, following the training regime she'd set herself.

The Maidstone charity run was one she had been looking forward to, a means to ease herself into running longer distances after a knee injury had put her out of action for most of the early part of the year.

It had been painful enough hobbling around at work, let alone trying to exercise when she got home.

Now though, she approached the T-junction and set her sights on the busy main road ahead, pausing a moment to check for oncoming traffic before hightailing it across to the pavement on the opposite side.

Her lungs were tightening now, and she forced herself to slow a little, to relax into a rhythm and breathe easily. This was a regular route for her, a shortened one compared to the elongated run she'd undertaken two nights ago.

Several of her colleagues were planning to run in the charity event, and she had no wish to embarrass herself in front of them.

Especially Amber Holstein.

A truck rumbled past her in the opposite direction, a motorbike following in its wake. In the distance, a police siren rang out from the other side of town and sent a shiver down her spine.

An uneasiness had gripped her since leaving the housing estate where she lived, and now she realised what had been bothering her.

Where she would normally see one or two familiar faces on her route, there was no-one out exercising.

She passed a solitary dog-walker with a black Labrador, the animal being gently berated as it took a distinct interest in a hedgerow, but that was it.

There were no other joggers in sight.

Not a single runner passed her.

A prickle of fear crept across her shoulders, and she picked up her pace as she reached the next junction.

She entered the winding road that snaked through the suburb and headed for home, her trainers pounding the pavement in a steady beat that matched her heart rate.

How were they going to stop a killer who was terrorising the community and had people fearing for their lives?

Ten minutes later, out of breath, she paused at the bottom of the staircase as the door to the ground floor flat opened and a woman in her early twenties peered out, dark eyes sparkling.

'I thought it might be you. Mum sent over too much food as usual – do you want some?'

Kay let out a relieved sigh. 'You're a star, Jasmina. I wouldn't say no, thanks. I haven't had a chance to get to the supermarket this week yet.'

Her neighbour's face clouded before she stood to one side to let Kay in, then closed the door. 'Are you working on that murder investigation? The two joggers?'

'Yeah.' She raised her gaze to the ceiling as loud foot-falls crossed the flat above before a door slammed. 'Thank God he works night shifts.'

Jasmina laughed, holding out a Tupperware box. 'Nothing wrong with a Bruce Willis film now and again.'

'Now and again being the operative words. Thanks for this – I thought something smelled good earlier.'

'Honestly, I'd rather have had a pizza, but you know Mum. She worries I might be starving. Do you fancy catching up for a drink later this week?'

'I'd love to, if I can. When does your shift at the surgery finish this week?'

'Six, usually, but I'll get an early finish on Friday.'

'Not catching up with Peter for dinner?'

'He's going out with the football team after practice.' Jasmina wrinkled her nose. 'There's only so much chat about the Premier League I can take.'

Kay laughed as she wandered back to the door. 'Then yes, let's try to get out for a drink.'

'Give me a call once you know what's happening at work.'

'Will do.' Kay crossed to the staircase. 'Thanks again for this.'

'No problem. And, Kay?'

She paused on the first step. 'Yes?'

'Be careful out there, all right?'

Chapter Four

The next morning, Kay peered through the passenger window as the pool car passed through the town centre, her gaze tracing the steady lines of commuters hurrying from the bus stops and train stations towards their places of work.

Beside her, Higgins rested his hands on the steering wheel while his fingers tapped along to a song he hummed under his breath, before he eased into a right-hand turn and pointed at a sign fixed to a lamp post.

'The gym's up here on the left. Do you know this one?'

'No – I cancelled my gym membership after Easter.' She sighed. 'It was getting too expensive, and I was hardly there. I tend to run these days.'

Higgins glanced across at her, then back to the road. 'I heard someone say you were into your running. Are you training for the charity race this weekend?'

'I'm trying to, in between working on this investigation.' She shuffled in her seat to face him. 'I went for a run last night when I got home. It was weird – there was hardly anyone else around. Blokes, yes – but no women. There are usually three or four who run at the same time as me in the evenings who I always say hello to.'

'These murders have them all spooked,' he said, his lip curling. 'The sooner we find out who's responsible…'

'Still think it's the same person?'

'That's my gut feel.'

'Me too. But, why? What's the connection between the two of them? There's been nothing to suggest they knew each other from the witness statements I've read.'

Higgins turned into a small car park beside a low-slung building and ratcheted the handbrake before pointing to the sign above the double doors. 'I don't know, but I guess we start here.'

McDowell's gym was a privately-owned establishment in one of the more affluent suburbs of the town, its front windows adorned with posters showing smiling models on stationary bikes, lifting weights or posing on rowing machines.

Kay scowled at the pictures as she passed, wondering if anyone in real life ever resembled one of the models after a sixty-minute spin class, and led the way through the doors into the reception area.

A stocky man in his forties with broad shoulders and closely-cropped brown hair looked up from a computer, then frowned as he realised he wouldn't be signing up two new members that morning.

'Dean McDowell,' he said, rising to his feet and shoving his hands in the pockets of his faded jeans. 'Can I help you?'

She noted the logo emblazoned across the front of his T-shirt. 'Are you the owner?'

'That's right.'

After holding up her warrant card and making the introductions, Kay leaned on the counter and gestured to the computer. 'We were wondering if you could confirm that Laura Scott was a member here.'

'Hang on,' he said and jabbed at the keys while squinting at the screen. 'Yes. Joined a couple of years ago, but doesn't attend many classes apart from Pilates by the look of it. I think she and a mate of hers use the sauna a couple of times a week, and I've seen her using the weights room at weekends.'

'That friend of hers—'

'Tanya Green, according to this log.'

'Right, thanks.' Kay tapped her fingers on the counter. 'What about Sarah Anderson – did she come here?'

McDowell clicked through his database, then shook his head. 'No-one here by that name. She was murdered too, wasn't she? Do you think they knew each other?'

'Too early to say, Mr McDowell. We're simply trying to establish known facts at the present time.'

Higgins cleared his throat, and she glanced across to where he stood next to a corkboard. He jerked his thumb over his shoulder at a poster that lifted in the breeze from the air conditioning vent above his head.

Kay recognised the logo for the charity run, then turned back to McDowell.

'Do you know how many members of your gym might be training for that?' she said.

He shrugged. 'Half a dozen, maybe. There might be

more – some people don't like to broadcast their training goals in case they don't achieve them, or change their minds.'

'Could you let me have a list of the members you know are planning to run?'

His eyes widened. 'Do you think they're in danger?'

'It's just a precaution,' said Kay. 'We'd like to speak with them, so if you have phone numbers and email addresses as well, I'd appreciate it.'

'Sure.' McDowell peered at his screen and wrote down the details before giving the piece of paper to her with a shaking hand.

'Thank you.' Kay tucked the page into her notebook, then raised her chin. 'One final thing, Mr McDowell. Where were you between the hours of three o'clock and seven o'clock yesterday morning?'

McDowell swallowed. 'I was at home asleep until the alarm went off at five, then I came in here and worked out until it was time to open at six-thirty.'

'Can anyone vouch for you?'

'My wife will, and we've got CCTV cameras all around the building – you'll see me on those.'

'Thank you, Mr McDowell.' Kay snapped shut her notebook. 'That will be all.'

Chapter Five

Kay hurried across Jubilee Square, then slowed as she approached Gabriel's Hill, wary of the cobblestones under her low heels and determined not to wrench her ankle.

It'd be sheer bad luck if she injured herself before the charity run and after last night's training session left her with sore calves, she was determined to up the ante on her regime.

Leaving the incident room to buy a cheap sandwich, she had paused on the way back at a favourite franchise and purchased coffee for herself and Higgins, grateful that the police constable had offered to make phone calls to the people on Dean McDowell's list of runners while she had fought her way through another list generated by calls to the Crimestoppers number set up for the enquiry.

They were winning the relentless battle with information by the time Sharp had commented on her stomach rumbling and told her to take a break – and the takeout coffee was better than the stuff in the vending machine outside the incident room.

Kay huffed her fringe out of her eyes and bit back a sense of frustration at the lack of progress.

Her mobile phone began to vibrate in her bag, and she paused to switch both takeout cups to one hand before rummaging in the side pocket and pressing the answer button before it went to voicemail.

'Hunter.'

'Only me.'

She recognised Higgins' voice and moved to the side of the pavement out of the way of an oncoming gaggle of teenagers in school uniforms. 'I'll be back in a sec. I'm nearly there.'

'I guessed that, but I've been told to head over to Headquarters – they need cover over there for the rest of the shift.'

Kay eyed the hot drinks in her hand. 'Who gets your coffee?'

Higgins chuckled. 'Best give it to Sharp. Might keep you in his good books.'

'Very funny. Okay, what d'you need?'

'Just thought I'd give you an update before I disappear. I've finished speaking with the members of McDowell's gym who Dean said had signed up for the charity run – only one of them knew Laura by sight but confirms he never ran with her. He and his wife live out Coxheath way and tend to train together or run with the local harriers' group every now and again. None of the others knew her or Sarah Anderson, and I've got alibis for all of them too. They all check out.'

Kay sighed. 'Okay. Worth a shot, anyway.'

'Hopefully, I'll be back in the morning – got to go.'

'Thanks, Higgins.'

She ended the call, dropped her phone back in her bag and picked up her pace as her thoughts tumbled over each other.

Making a mental note to check that one of her colleagues had spoken to Laura's neighbours about her running habits and whether she had been seen leaving her house yesterday morning with anyone, Kay zig-zagged between the stationary traffic on Palace Avenue and sidled through the security gates to the police station as they opened to let a liveried patrol car out.

It paused next to her, the window lowering before an arm snaked out.

'I'll take it with me.'

She leaned in and handed over the coffee to Higgins. 'Sharp will be gutted he's missing out.'

'Don't tell him.'

Kay laughed as he pulled away, then frowned as she saw two figures emerge from a silver four-door vehicle at the far end of the car park.

Amber grinned at Kay as she drew closer. 'Hi, Hunter! How's your training going?'

'Okay, I suppose,' Kay said, then took a sip of coffee.

'Oh, I wouldn't drink that stuff if I were you.' Amber wrinkled her nose. 'You'll dehydrate too fast – you need to stick to non-caffeinated herbal tea at the moment. That's what my personal trainer advises, anyway.'

'I'll bear that in mind, thanks.'

Hugh peered over his shoulder at the sound of her voice as he lifted a briefcase from the back seat, and Kay raised her chin so she could look him in the eye.

'I'd listen to her if I were you,' he said. 'Amber's hoping for a decent race against you on Saturday.'

Despite her natural competitiveness, Kay paused beside the lithe assistant forensic technician.

'You are taking all this seriously, aren't you, Amber? Making sure you don't run on your own, that sort of thing while we try to catch this bastard, I mean.'

The forensic assistant laughed. 'Oh, don't worry about me. I always make sure I run in a pair, anyway – it makes for a better training regime because I've got someone to pace with. You should try it sometime,' she added before turning on her heel and making her way over to the entrance to the police station.

Hugh swung shut the car door, aiming the key fob at the vehicle before grimacing at Kay.

'I really don't fancy your chances against her, Hunter.'

'Thanks a lot, Hugh.'

'Well, just so you know – there's a sweepstake going around the office.' He shrugged. 'Her odds are better than yours.'

Kay's mouth dropped open as he hurried after his colleague.

'Bloody great,' she muttered, then glanced at her watch and swore.

The briefing was due to start in five minutes.

Chapter Six

Kay leaned her head against the bus window and watched the darkening Tonbridge skyline come into view, cursing the broken clutch that meant her car was in for repair, leaving her to rely on public transport that day.

The journey home took thirty-five minutes by train, but due to signalling works she was corralled onto a bus replacement service at Maidstone.

She swayed on her feet for the first few miles, hanging on to the back of a seat and jostling for elbow space with a crowd of disgruntled commuters, turning her face away from a large man with body odour as he'd leered at her.

Sinking into a spare seat at Wateringbury as soon as a woman rose to leave, Kay plucked the free newspaper she left behind and began flicking through the pages.

Most of it was regurgitated celebrity gossip, interspersed with a little news and advertisements for local businesses.

Her gaze wandered over the bright coloured boxes extolling the cost benefits of having her legs waxed ('A

Massive 20% Off!') alongside the option of visiting a psychologist if Kay was over-stressed or trying to quit smoking (Kay wasn't, on both counts) until she turned the page, and stopped.

Kay swallowed and re-read the brightly-coloured print.

A split second later, her heart jumped.

Underneath a feature about the upcoming charity run, an advertisement had been placed.

Surrounded by a bright red border, the wording leapt from the page, taunting her.

Get the best from your training. Download our free app. Map your route. Compare your times. Race your friends!

Below the wording, the advertisement reference had been displayed, together with a website address. No phone number.

Kay checked over her shoulder. The bus was empty now, save for a teenager listening to music at the far end, a faint *hiss-hiss* audible from where she sat.

She pulled out her phone, flicked to the front of the newspaper, and dialled the advertising manager's number, crossing her fingers that he'd be working late.

He was.

Kay identified herself, explained what she needed, and told him she'd be at his office with the relevant paperwork in the morning.

Chapter Seven

Her shift was three hours old by the time she'd found Higgins, explained he was coming with her for the day, assuring him she meant work, nothing else, and made her way across town to meet with the advertising manager of the free newspaper.

Chatting with the newspaper executive resulted in them being given the name and address of the man who had placed the advertisement and after she'd explained her theory to Sharp, he'd sent them away to investigate further.

Fifty-five minutes later, Higgins swung the car into a leafy cul-de-sac, slowed at the kerb, and turned off the engine.

They sat for a moment, eyeing up the properties on the small street.

The front gardens varied from being lovingly tended to the unfenced basics of the house in front of them.

'Background check confirms Cameron Ashe and his wife have been renting here for three months,' said

Higgins, his hands still on the steering wheel as he peered up at the bedroom windows. 'No kids. Moved down from Bolton.'

'Any pets?'

'No, so we don't have to worry about dogs attacking us.'

'Just as well. Right, let's do this,' Kay said, opening her door. 'And if you think of anything I need to ask about this app of his and I don't raise it, feel free to chime in.'

'Will do.'

After Higgins rang the doorbell, they stood on the front step for a couple of minutes before the door swung open, and a thin man of medium height peered out at them through bloodshot eyes.

His hair awry, he frowned, tucked his stained T-shirt into his jeans, the pushed his glasses back up his nose.

'Can I help you?'

Kay introduced Higgins and herself before she held up the newspaper clipping. 'Mr Ashe – can you please confirm you placed this advertisement?'

He squinted, reached out and pulled her hand closer, then nodded. 'Yes, I did. What's this about?'

Kay lowered the newspaper. 'Could we come in, sir?'

'Sure, sure.'

He turned and led the way into a sparsely furnished living area, the paintwork beige and the carpet threadbare. Within six paces, he'd reached the kitchen worktops and turned back to them.

'Did you want tea or anything?'

'No, thanks – that won't be necessary,' Kay said.

'We'd like to ask you some questions about your running app.'

He nodded. 'Okay. Why don't you come through to the office, then?'

With that, he opened the back door and walked outside.

Kay turned to Higgins, raised an eyebrow, and then followed Ashe.

They traipsed across an overgrown garden until they caught up with him outside a cinderblock shed.

He turned to them, his hand on the door handle. 'The last place we rented had an office in the house. Best we could afford down here was this. It's warm and dry, though.'

He flicked on a switch as he led the way into the small space, and a fluorescent strip light blinked into life above their heads. He waved them onto two packing cases next to his desk, while he sat on a battered office chair.

The desk was a simple set-up – computer and screen, three drawers under the desk, and a filing tray rack next to the computer hard drive.

Ashe rubbed his hands on his thighs as they lowered themselves into their makeshift seats, and Kay nodded to Higgins as he pulled out his notebook and pen.

After Ashe had given them the potted history of how he'd left school, joined an IT company, then left that to pursue a career writing apps for smartphones a year ago, Kay brought his attention back to the newspaper advertisement.

'So, this running app,' Kay said. 'From what I understand, it records people's routes, and they can keep track of their times and see how they're improving, right?'

'Yes.'

'Do you pass on that information to any third parties?'

'No, that's not allowed,' he said. 'There are strict data protection laws against doing that.'

'But you do collect the data?'

'Yes.'

'Can you show me?'

'Of course. Hang on.'

He spun around on his chair, then wiggled the mouse on the desk until the computer burst to life.

Kay watched, his movements swift and precise as he brought up the programme on the screen. She stood, moving closer until she was standing at his shoulder and could see what he was doing.

'This is the background part of the app programme,' he explained. 'All the users' information is stored here.'

'What sort of data do you collect?'

'Names, addresses, credit card details – for updates,' he explained. 'And then we keep records of their routes, including their favourite ones, personal best times, and any other training data they want to record.'

'Why collect so much information if you don't intend to pass it on to third parties?' asked Higgins.

Kay held her thumb up to him behind Ashe's back, lowering her hand as the IT expert turned.

'In case users lose their running data,' he said. 'We provide a full back-up service with the app, so if users lose their phone or change it, we can transfer the data over for them.'

'Is it possible, then, for you to monitor, say, one particular runner's progress over time?' Kay asked. 'Just by analysing the historical data the app records?'

'Yes. We don't use it, but the coding programme is set up to be able to do that.'

Kay's head jerked up at the sound of a gate being slammed shut and footsteps in the yard outside.

'Ah, that'll be my wife, Cheryl,' said Ashe, standing.

Kay glanced at Higgins, and then watched as Ashe moved to the door.

'I'm in here, love.'

A petite redhead appeared in the doorway, her long hair tied back in a ponytail, her arms and legs muscular and tanned, poking out from designer-labelled running shorts and a T-shirt.

Kay sensed her own calf muscles grow flabbier as she looked at her.

There was nothing like meeting a serious athlete when you were several weeks behind on your own training regime.

'Cheryl does all the book-keeping for the business,' Ashe explained after introducing them.

'I work part-time a couple of days a week and then look after Cameron's business the rest of the time in between training,' Cheryl added, flicking her hair over her shoulder and brushing her palm over her forehead to slick away imaginary sweat.

'And you did this in Bolton as well?'

He nodded. 'Yes. Cheryl missed the warmer weather down here, though, so we decided to move back a few months ago.' His nose wrinkled as he glanced around at the meagre office space. 'Hopefully, the business will grow, and we can afford a place of our own soon.'

Kay nodded to Higgins. 'I think we're done here, Constable Higgins.' Kay turned to Ashe and his wife. 'Thank you for your time, Mr Ashe. Can you confirm the telephone number we can reach you on if we have further questions?'

'Sure.' He moved past her, leaned across the desk, and scribbled on a notepad before tearing out the page and handing it to her.

'Thank you.' Kay turned to Cheryl. 'Do you use your husband's app for your training?'

She laughed. 'Oh no – I don't understand smartphones at all,' she said. 'I've still got one of those old flip-open ones. It makes phone calls and sends texts. That's it.'

'Cheryl's a great book-keeper, but all the technology stuff goes over her head, doesn't it, love?' Ashe smiled, putting his arm around his wife's waist.

She smiled at him before turning her attention back to Kay.

'He's right, it does. I haven't got a clue.'

Chapter Eight

'Do you know what I think? I reckon that after he's got all the information from the app, he can analyse it to find out where women are running, what times they run at, and how fast they run.'

Kay finished talking and waited while Sharp scribbled on the whiteboard, re-capped the pen, and picked up his coffee.

'So, routine is their killer, is that what you're saying?' asked Higgins.

Kay turned in her seat to face her colleague and leaned an arm over the back. 'Exactly, and he's using the app to track their movements. I know what I'm like when I'm out for a run – I have favourite routes, especially since I've been training for the charity race.'

'Then we know how to draw him out, don't we, Hunter?'

Kay turned at the sound of Sharp's voice. Her eyes widened as her thought processes caught up.

'Really?' Her eyes narrowed. 'How?'

'I executed a search warrant based on your report, and we've used that to request a copy of Ashe's database. We know all the routes his users take. All we need now is someone capable of running those routes.'

'You can't be serious.'

He folded his arms across his chest. 'I'm very serious,' he said, his smile disappearing. 'I think you've made a valid case for your theory. And we're out of time.' He pointed to the calendar on the wall. 'The charity run is on Saturday. If we don't catch him before then, based on your theory, we might lose him for good – because he'll move on. There isn't another race scheduled in this area until June.'

Her shoulders slumped.

'Kay.' Sharp crossed the space between them. He reached out and patted her shoulder, then pointed at the whiteboard. 'We'll be there with you. Based on what evidence we've got, we now know the sort of person he targets, and we can work out where the grab points are in each park.'

'We'll need to contact the women on that database,' Kay said. 'Advise them to stay away from their usual routes and stop using the app until we've got him in custody.'

'Higgins can do that while we're setting up the operation,' said Sharp, clicking his fingers at the young constable.

Kay sighed. She knew he was right. 'I just feel uncomfortable being used as bait.'

A frown creased Sharp's brow before he spoke. 'At

Rachel Amphlett

least you know what you're getting into,' he said. 'Those two women didn't.'

Kay closed her eyes, ashamed. 'Yes, Sarge.'

He moved away, gathered up the files on his desk and turned towards the door. 'I'll bring the DI up to speed on our proposal.' He opened the door and paused. 'Good work, detective.'

Kay managed a small smile before he stalked from the room.

Chapter Nine

Her legs ached, her thighs burned, and Kay knew her face was beetroot red because even the sweat running down it was warm.

'Just another lap to go.' Sharp's voice fizzled through her earpiece.

Kay could hear laughter in the background and cursed them all while her shoes pounded the concrete bike path.

The sun had disappeared over the horizon an hour ago, and as soon as Sharp had received confirmation from the Kent Police IT experts that they'd hacked the app and set up a new account for her, including a month-long running history, they set out to catch their killer.

In her other ear, the running app counted off the distance, a calm and collected female voice belonging to someone who, in Kay's opinion, had never run in her life.

'Okay, you're hitting the last two hundred metres,' said Sharp. 'Slow to a walk, and look exhausted.'

Kay choked out a response, slowed as he suggested,

and walked until she found a bench she could stretch against.

A street lamp cast a pyramid of light around her, confining the surrounding parkland to darkness.

She forced down the panic that threatened to have her running in the opposite direction within seconds.

Instead, starting with her aching calf muscles, Kay began to stretch. She worked her way up until she was flexing her arms across her chest, and had just raised her hands above her head when the hairs on the back of her neck stood on end.

She cried out as Ashe emerged from the bushes behind the wooden seat, his hands in the pockets of his dark coloured jacket.

'Detective Hunter,' he said, ambling closer. 'I was hoping I'd see you here.'

Kay swallowed, Sharp's voice in her earpiece shouting, mobilising the team towards her position.

'Mr Ashe,' Kay spluttered. She coughed a couple of times to clear her throat and tried again. 'Hello – what are you doing here?'

'Don't run away.'

'What do you mean?'

He came closer. 'It's all right,' he said. 'I only wanted to talk to you.'

Kay narrowed her eyes. 'I gave you my business card. You could have called me at the station or left a message for me.'

'It's much better if we talk here. Away from prying eyes.'

'I really don't think that's a good idea,' Kay said, backing away.

He held up his hand. 'No – really, I just want to talk.'

He drew closer, a desperate look in his eyes, and a small smile etched across his lips.

Kay caught movement in her peripheral vision and jerked her arm away, Ashe's fingers brushing against her skin.

'Please – we need to talk,' he urged.

'Don't touch me,' Kay hissed, backing away.

'It's okay. I won't hurt you,' he said. 'Shall we sit down?'

'No.'

'Please,' he said. 'It'll only take a minute, I promise.'

She fought down the urge to put into practice the self-defence training she'd received at the refresher course only two months ago, instead of giving him the impression she was weak. She took a step backwards.

Ashe lurched towards her with both arms open wide.

'No! Leave me alone!'

Her cries were cut short by a series of shouts – voices from the dark parkland behind her and further along the bike path.

Kay moved fast, blocking Ashe's escape back into the bushes, trying to make her slight frame intimidating.

Ashe spun round to face her, his face stricken. 'Don't do this – you're making a terrible mistake!'

'I don't think so,' Kay gasped as a dark shape pushed past her.

Higgins launched his body at Ashe, pulling the man to

the ground, sending both of them tumbling into the long grass behind the bench.

As Higgins pulled the software engineer to his feet, Sharp slid to a stop next to her.

'Are you okay?'

Kay nodded. 'I think so, Sarge. He scared me.'

'You did good,' said Sharp. 'Let's go back to the station and see what he has to say for himself.'

Chapter Ten

When Kay walked through the door into the observation room, she saw that DC Richard Christie had joined Sharp in interview room two, his pen hovering over his notepad.

On screen, at the table opposite two detectives and with a duty solicitor beside him, Ashe groaned and held his head in his hands, keeping his gaze lowered.

Kay put down her coffee cup, leaned forward and turned up the volume.

'Interview commences at eight forty-two,' said Sharp, pushing the record button on the machine next to him, and then indicating to the detective constable beside him to begin.

'First of all, Mr Ashe, we'd like to know why you were following our colleague in the park tonight?' Christie narrowed his eyes. 'Why did you approach her?'

Heat rose to the other man's face under the detectives' scrutiny. 'I-I was testing a new update to the app, that's all. I happened to see her, and I wondered if perhaps I might be able to help with your investigation.'

'In what way?'

'Well, I thought if we told female runners in the area that the new update enables them to share their route with their friends in real-time, rather than retrospectively like the old version, it'd help them.' Ashe looked from Christie to Sharp. 'It's a safety feature, you see? They wouldn't feel like they were running alone.'

'Hardly appropriate to accost one of our officers at night with a marketing spiel,' said Sharp.

'So, Mr Ashe,' said Christie. 'How long have you been tracking your victims using your software?'

'I haven't, I swear.'

'Is this why you had to move from Bolton two months ago?'

Sharp leaned across the desk. 'Tell us, Ashe,' he said. 'If we phone our colleagues up in Lancashire, are we going to hear a similar story to our two murders?'

Ashe sighed and raised his head. 'It's not what you think.'

Christie turned at a knock at the door, his concentration broken.

Higgins appeared. 'Apologies for interrupting, Sarge, but could I have a word?'

'Interview paused at eight-fifty,' said Sharp, hitting the stop button.

Christie followed him through the door and closed it behind him.

Kay shot from her seat, reaching the corridor outside at the same time as the two detectives.

'What is it?'

Higgins glanced from her to Sharp, and then back, before drawing a long breath.

'There's been another murder,' he said. 'In a park two miles from where we picked up Mr Ashe.'

Kay blinked, the corridor lights suddenly too bright.

'When?'

'The body was discovered by a dog walker twenty minutes ago,' said Higgins. 'The call's only just been routed through to us from Headquarters.'

Sharp's shoulders sagged.

'All right, Christie,' he said. 'Let's get back in there and tell Mr Ashe he'll be staying with us for a while yet. Then we'll go to the scene.'

'Shall I drive, Sarge?' said Kay.

The detective sergeant paused with his hand on the door to the interview room, then glanced over his shoulder. 'No need, Kay. Get yourself home. It's been a long day.'

Kay bit her lip as the door closed behind the two men, and rubbed her arms before walking back to the incident room, her stomach churning.

Another woman dead, and it was all her fault.

Chapter Eleven

Kay aimed the remote controller at the television and jabbed at the buttons.

Her running shoes sat next to the front door and from the kitchen, she could hear the washing machine on its final spin as the theme tune to a murder mystery series began to ring out.

She sighed at the screen, switched the channel and threw the remote onto a small wooden table next to her feet before picking up the large glass of red she'd poured ten minutes ago.

A half-eaten Chinese takeaway sat next to her mobile phone, the prawn dish growing cold as her appetite waned.

No-one had said anything to her when she collected her bag and coat from the incident room, but she could sense them all looking at her.

Sharp had passed her at the bottom of the stairs, ignoring her as he raised his mobile phone to his ear. It was DC Christie who told her Cameron Ashe had been released, pending further enquiries.

Face reddening, Kay had scuttled out of the back door of the police station and up the hill to the bus stop, sure that her fellow travellers could sense her embarrassment.

She eyed the leftover takeaway and wondered if it would keep until the next night.

Chances were, she was in for some more late shifts.

Her mobile phone vibrated on the table, and she groaned at the name displayed on the screen before answering.

'Hello, Mum.'

'You sound tired.'

It was an accusation, not an observation. Her mother's voice held no warmth, no concern, and Kay winced at the harsh pitch.

'I'm fine. Long day, that's all.'

'I knew you weren't cut out for this sort of thing,' her mother scolded. 'It's not too late to do something else with your life, you know. You're only twenty-seven.'

'Did you want something?'

'Can't I call to see how you are?'

'I'm okay.'

'Not by the sound of it. Why don't you find a nice job? Something nine to five that will give you a chance to have a bit of a social life? You haven't had a boyfriend in ages, have you?'

Kay said nothing, although her gaze wandered to the bouquet of flowers on the bookcase next to the television.

'How's Dad?' she managed.

'Down the pub playing darts. I don't know why – he needs to lose weight. I keep telling him it's not healthy to go down there all the time. He says it's to give me some peace and quiet…'

Kay rolled her eyes. 'Mum, I've got to go. Busy day tomorrow, and I'm due in early.'

'That's what I'm saying, Kay. Find something else to do. Something you're good at…'

Kay ended the call while her mother was in the middle of saying her goodbyes and tossed aside the phone.

'Bloody hell,' she mumbled and wiped tears of frustration from her cheeks.

Three months since her training had ended, and she could feel her initial confidence and excitement ebbing away.

She had been so sure that Ashe was their suspect, so sure that his app was the link between the murders, that she had made a catastrophic mistake and caused another woman's death.

She sniffed, then picked up her wineglass and padded through to the kitchen, topping it up with the last of the Shiraz before re-capping the bottle.

She set it down with a clatter on the worktop and blinked.

What if the murders weren't connected?

How on earth were they going to catch a killer who murdered at random?

Chapter Twelve

The next morning, Kay swiped her security card over the panel beside the reception desk and held open the door for a pair of uniformed constables, their arms laden with cardboard boxes.

They raced up the stairs leading to the incident rooms, their boots thumping across the thin carpet when they reached the floor above.

'What's all that about?' she said.

'A raid over at Paddock Wood. Money laundering or something,' said Sergeant Maurice Hoyle. He turned away from the reception desk and rested his arm on the counter. 'Are you all right? You had a face like thunder when you left here last night.'

'Bad day.'

'Ah. I heard a suspect was released last night – was he one of yours?'

'I thought he was our killer.'

The older sergeant's face softened. 'And then someone else died, right?'

She nodded.

'I hope someone told you it wasn't your fault,' he said.

'That doesn't make it any better.'

'No, but it does give you a reason to get upstairs and get back to work, doesn't it? They're not going to catch the real killer without you. All hands on deck, and all that.'

Kay forced a smile and patted her fist against the door frame. 'Speaking of which, I should get going.'

'Before you do, I overheard Higgins saying that you were worrying about your training for the charity run with everything else going on.'

'Just a bit.' She sighed. 'I said to him yesterday that I went out for a run on my own the other night, and there was hardly anyone else around. I don't see myself using that app any time soon, either.'

'You should do what my wife does – she belongs to a running group on social media. They arrange to go out in pairs, especially at the moment. If they do prefer to run alone then they post their route and what time they expect to be back so if they don't check in on their return, someone can raise the alarm for them.' He smiled. 'Of course, it's not all serious – they post their progress as well, best times, things like that. Sophie enjoys it because it keeps her motivated, and it keeps me happy because someone always knows where she is.'

He reached out for a piece of paper and scrawled across it. 'This is the group. All you do is send them a request to join and someone will approve it. I'll tell Sophie to keep a look out for you if you like.'

'Thanks, Maurice – appreciate it. I'll take a look later.'

Kay hurried up the stairs and into the incident room,

switching on her computer while she shrugged her arms out of her coat before hanging it over the back of her chair.

A general hubbub of noise filled the space, and despite the paranoia seeping through her thoughts none of her colleagues had seized upon the chance to tease her about her error the night before.

Instead, grim faces peered at computer screens while phones rang, and urgent conversations swept over her as she worked her way through her emails and the tasks that were delegated to her through the Home Office Large Major Enquiry System.

It was going to be a busy day.

Chapter Thirteen

'I got you cheese and tomato – that all right?'

Kay looked up from her computer screen at the sound of DC Christie's voice, and stifled a yawn.

'Brilliant, thanks, Rich.'

He handed her the wrapped sandwich then pulled across a spare chair, the casters rattling over a protective rubber mat placed under the desk by the previous occupant.

'How're you doing?'

'All right,' she said between mouthfuls. She swallowed, then pointed at the screen. 'I've cross-referenced the gyms again, but our third victim – Alicia Martin – hadn't been to the gym she belonged to in over four months.'

'Any idea why?'

'The owner there said it's common – people join up in the New Year and get all excited about a new routine before they start to drift away. He reckons memberships like that cover his overheads for six months.'

Christie grimaced. 'I think the bloke who owns my local gym would say the same thing.'

Kay reached into her tray and pulled out a folder full of witness statements. 'I've been reading through the statements uniform took last night, too. None of the property owners along that stretch of footpath heard anything or saw anything suspicious. If it wasn't for that dog-walker...'

'Alicia might've lain there all night before she was discovered.' Christie pushed his chair back and rose, straightening his jacket. 'Good work, anyway.'

'Rich?' Kay scrunched up the empty sandwich wrapper in her hand and took a deep breath. 'I'm sorry about yesterday. I screwed up.'

'No, you didn't. It was a valid lead, and it needed to be actioned. You did the right thing in the circumstances. Ashe wasn't exactly acting rationally by approaching you in the park, either so...'

'But Alicia—'

'Would've died anyway. We had nothing to suggest she was going to be the next victim – or any other suspects.' He gave the chair a shove, sending it to a shuddering standstill under the neighbouring desk. 'What would you have done in Sharp's shoes if someone had come to you with the same information?'

Kay exhaled. 'Acted on it.'

'There you go, then.' He winked. 'Don't stay too late tonight. We need you bright-eyed and bushy-tailed back here in the morning.'

Chapter Fourteen

Despite Christie's advice, the incident room was almost deserted by the time Kay looked at the time on her computer screen and realised it was seven o'clock.

Beyond the windows, a light fog smudged the orange glow from sodium streetlights and somewhere within the building, a vacuum cleaner hummed as the cleaners worked.

'Night, Kay.' Higgins held up his hand as he walked towards the door, a black backpack slung over one shoulder.

'Night.'

She scrolled the mouse over the screen, closing different apps and windows, and wondered whether to find somewhere to have dinner in town before heading home or order a takeaway.

She groaned. A takeaway two nights in a row, and her race on Saturday would suffer.

Unless she went for a run before heading home – she

kept a spare pair of trainers and clothes in her locker downstairs.

Decision made, she reached out to turn off her computer and then froze.

The piece of paper Maurice handed to her that morning was tucked under her desk phone, the name of the social media group stark under the harsh office lighting.

Kay glanced over her shoulder.

The incident room was empty now, Higgins being the only one who had stayed behind so he could enter the last of the phone enquiries received that afternoon into the HOLMES database.

Her eyes fell on the calendar next to her computer screen.

The charity run was only three days away, and Alicia's murder had taken place within three days of Laura's.

There had been a week between Laura's murder and the first.

Were the murders getting closer together because the race date was drawing near?

Was someone else going to die tonight?

Heart racing, she hurried over to the whiteboard at the far end of the room, swearing under her breath as her leg struck the corner of a colleague's desk in her haste to reach it.

Rubbing her thigh, she ran her eyes over the map, the pins denoting where the victims were found, and the red marker pen lines that Sharp had added to highlight the area where the killer appeared to be operating.

It was a few miles in diameter, but it would do.

Kay returned to her desk, threw herself into her chair and pulled her keyboard towards her.

She clicked on the internet browser on her screen, logged in to the social media site, and searched for running groups in the town.

Maurice's wife's group was one of the top results, but Kay avoided that.

She needed to find one whose members ran in the same area where the three victims were found, and she needed to act fast.

Kay scrolled through the list of four groups, clicking on each and then discarding the link when she found the group's members lived outside of the killer's circle.

She found the group she sought on her fifth attempt and sent a request to join.

It didn't take long.

A notification appeared in the top left of the screen within seconds.

Kay took a deep breath, then picked up her mobile phone and found Sharp's number.

It went straight to voicemail.

'Dammit.'

She tapped the phone against her chin for a moment, then dialled DC Christie's number.

Engaged.

Kay drummed her fingers on the desk.

Of course, they could be talking to each other – catching up before the morning's briefing. Or both of them could be talking to someone else.

She closed her eyes for a moment, then opened them and squared her shoulders.

This couldn't wait.

She clicked on a space on the social media group's main page to add a new post and introduced herself as someone new to the area – easy enough to do, as she was rarely on the site and her personal profile was set to private.

Going out for a run tonight – been too scared to lately but if I don't, I won't be ready for Saturday's race, she began.

She added the route she planned to take, then sat back and read through the words.

A predatory smile twitched at her lips.

I reckon if I train tonight and rest tomorrow, I'll easily be in the top three to finish – maybe I'll even win! she typed, and for good measure added a grinning emoji.

'That should work, you bastard.'

Chapter Fifteen

Kay rested her foot on a concrete bollard blocking vehicle access into the park and re-laced her shoes.

It gave her a chance to scan her surroundings, although the thickening fog meant she could only see a hundred metres in each direction.

The car park was deserted save for her own vehicle, a new clutch fitted and her bank account five hundred pounds lighter.

In the distance, she heard a solitary truck engine as its driver changed gear to counteract the steep climb up the hill past the park, the sound muffled by the fog.

Her breath misted as she took a gulp of air, exhaling to try to release some of the stress clutching at her limbs as she took in the muted outlines of trees lining the footpath, ghostly silhouettes against the streetlights overhead that struggled to pierce the gloom.

'Okay, Hunter,' she muttered, zipping up her car keys and mobile phone within her sweatshirt pockets. 'Enough stalling.'

She set herself an easy pace to begin with, the route clear in her mind.

The footpath made for smooth progress and when she glanced over her shoulder she was shocked to find she could no longer see her car.

Ahead, the path curved around to the left and away from the back gardens that bordered the park.

For the next half a mile, she would be alone.

She increased her stride, her leg muscles warming up and easing into the familiar training routine.

Any other time, she knew she would enjoy the chance to discover a new route but paranoia was already beginning to set in.

Should she have waited and tried again to phone Sharp and Christie?

Should she have posted the challenge to the killer in the first place?

She slowed to a walk, then stopped as the realisation hit her that she had no idea what she was going to do when or if she did confront the killer.

'Kay.'

She froze, peering into the gloom, her heart pounding. 'Who's there?'

A figure loomed out from the fog, moving closer from behind the abandoned swing set to her left and advancing towards her.

Kay took a step back, her mouth falling open at the sight of the familiar face.

'Amber? What're you doing here?'

Chapter Sixteen

'More to the point, Hunter – why are you here?'

The trainee crime scene technician stepped closer, then shrugged open her waterproof running jacket and pulled out a baseball bat.

Kay's eyes widened, and she held up her hands. 'I fancied a run after work, that's all. You?'

'You're a liar, Hunter.' Amber flicked her long blonde hair over her shoulder. 'Thought you'd try to catch a killer on your own, did you?'

Kay moved to the side and looked left and right but there was no-one else there.

No-one to save her.

She cursed at her own stupidity.

If she tried to scream, no-one would hear her.

The thick fog would deafen the sound, mask her cries for help.

'I can explain, Amber.'

'Go on, then.'

'I just wanted to try to stop anyone else getting hurt. I

thought if I could—'

'Set a trap? Catch a killer on your own?' Amber cocked her head to one side. 'Did you really think you were that good?'

'How did you know I'd be here?'

'That's *my* running group,' the woman hissed. 'Mine.'

Kay let out a shaking laugh. 'My God, that's it, isn't it? That's how you've been picking out your victims. Anyone who posts a better time than you, and you kill them.' She frowned. 'Why?'

'Because I can.' Amber swung the baseball bat against a rhododendron bush, sending leaves flying over the footpath. 'Because I like it. Because it stops anyone from beating me to the finish line.'

'You're sick,' said Kay, unable to keep the disgust from her voice.

Amber laughed and took another swipe at the plant.

'You need to get help,' said Kay. 'I can help you. We'll go to Sharp together…'

'No.' Amber spun around to face her, her eyes wild. 'You're not going anywhere.'

Kay took a step back and held up her hands, her mouth dry as she realised she'd miscalculated.

There would be no negotiation.

No making Amber see sense.

No way out.

The woman leapt forward, and Kay felt a dull ache against the side of her head as she turned to run.

She stumbled, scraping her hands on the stony ground as she fell, crying out as her ankle twisted.

'You had to be better, didn't you?' Amber sneered,

swinging the baseball bat from side to side. 'You couldn't help yourself, rubbing it in everyone's face that you were going to do so well this weekend, and poking around instead of minding your own business.'

Kay shuffled backwards, her elbows digging into the soft turf while her ankles tried to find purchase.

A darkness flashed across Amber's face then and she snarled, raising the baseball bat above her head.

'I'm better than you,' she spat. 'And now I always will be.'

Kay screamed and raised her arm as the bat swung down, then gasped as a shadow shot out from the fog and tackled Amber to the ground.

The baseball bat clattered to the footpath.

Kay pushed herself to her feet and bit back a cry as a jolt of pain shot through her leg.

Amber was shrieking as she punched and kicked at her assailant – but he was too strong for her.

He flipped her onto her stomach, then pinned her down with his knees and peered over his shoulder to where Kay stood, her mouth open in surprise.

'Hunter, for chrissakes,' he gasped. 'Handcuffs – back pocket.'

'Sarge?'

Chapter Seventeen

Kay winced as Higgins patted a cotton wool ball soaked in antiseptic lotion against the cuts on her face, then held up her hand to stop him as a familiar figure appeared at the open door to the observation room.

Hugh Hughes had aged since she'd last seen him, the crime scene investigator's face a sickly grey as he eyed the bruises forming on her arms.

'Kay, I'm so sorry – I had no idea. I—'

'None of us did, Hugh. It's okay.'

His shoulders slumped. 'Even so. There'll be an enquiry.'

'You weren't to blame for any of this. Have you spoken with Sharp?'

'Yes – he's just finished taking my formal statement. I'm about to head home, and then I expect I'll be asked to attend a professional hearing at some point.'

'She fooled us all, didn't she?'

'None more so than me, Kay. Sharp thinks she got a kick out of carrying out her victims' own crime scene investigations and trying to outsmart us.' He shivered. 'She's been working here for eight months. God knows how many more she's killed.'

'She'll be put away for a long time,' said Kay. 'We'll make sure of that.'

He gave her a sad smile. 'Look after yourself.'

Higgins turned to her as the pathologist left, his eyes wide. 'Bloody hell. Can't imagine what he's going through at the moment.'

'I know.' Kay yelped as he applied more antiseptic to a scratch above her eyebrow. 'And stop that – you're enjoying it too much.'

Chapter Eighteen

'Kay?'

She turned at the sound of Sharp's voice to see him hurrying down the stairs towards her.

'Sarge?'

He led her away from the front desk. 'Let's talk outside.'

Kay frowned, but fell into step beside him.

'Amber has confessed to the three murders,' he said. 'We found the victims' mobile phones in her locker. She deleted the posts they wrote in her social media group after she targeted them.'

Kay swallowed. 'Jesus, Sarge.'

He said nothing further as they headed out of the front door.

When they reached the kerb, he waited until two uniformed constables had passed, then turned to her.

'Don't ever take a risk like that again, Kay.'

'I tried to phone you, Sarge. And Richard. Both of your phones were engaged.'

'You should've waited.'

'I'm sorry, Sarge, but I was worried if I did, we'd miss the opportunity and he'd kill again.'

'He very nearly did. If it wasn't for the fact my wife Rebecca follows the same social media group that you posted in and told me what you wrote in there—'

Kay blinked, the realisation smacking her in the chest.

'I've taken the liberty of ordering a taxi for you,' Sharp said. 'It's late, and I don't want you travelling on public transport. Not with a twisted ankle, and not after what you've been through tonight. I'll have someone fetch your car for you and bring it back here.'

'Okay, thanks.'

He nodded, then scuffed the toe of his shoe against the bottom step, his hands in his pockets.

Eventually, he spoke.

'Look, one day you'll be in my shoes,' said Sharp, 'and you'll be telling your team the same thing, believe me. Don't risk your life – or that of your colleagues. It might be one of us who has to deal with the aftermath.'

'I understand.'

He nodded, then turned as a taxi pulled up to the kerb. 'Here's your ride – and here's twenty quid towards the fare.'

'Sarge, you don't have to do that.'

Sharp grinned and held open the passenger door for her.

'Trust me, I do. At least that way, I know you'll get home safe.'

Kay smiled as she got in, then wound down the window.

'Thanks, Sarge. For everything. See you tomorrow.'

THE END

About the Author

Rachel Amphlett is a USA Today bestselling author of crime fiction and spy thrillers, many of which have been translated worldwide.

Her novels are available in eBook, print, and audiobook formats from libraries and retailers as well as her website shop.

A keen traveller, Rachel has both Australian and British citizenship.

Find out more about Rachel's books at:
www.rachelamphlett.com